Immaculate

The second novel of the Touched series

by

L. G. Boyle

Rachel
God bless!
Loria

For Mama Bessie
You instilled in me a love of reading His Word.

Acknowledgements

I remain thankful to God for surrounding me with a host of family and friends. Between them, they have provided a deep well of love, encouragement and unwavering support from which I draw, unabashedly, in times of need. Special thanks to my son, Larrie, and to my daughter, Loreah, who both stand beside me in pictures and in real life. A debt of gratitude is owed to my sister, Norvella, my proofreader and number one fan and to my brother, George, who has always been my rock, friend, and confidante. And a shout out to all who received my debut novel well and clamored for the sequel to *Touched*. This story is for you.

"... and, lo, the star,
which they saw in the east,
went before them,
till it came and stood over
where the young child was."

Matthew 2:9

Prologue

Sulayman

... stood overlooking his kingdom. His lands stretched before him with his people working below. Some tended sheep and goats while prodding them with sharp sticks. Others kept their plots of vegetables, which were laid out in neat rows. Sulayman saw those who had dedicated their lives to service, ministering before the God of their fathers, day and night. There were those, also, who guarded the contents of their Temple and kept its holy relics and secrets. Precious items were held within that, should they be discovered, might bring joy to some and dismay to others. The news of their survival might even start a war over their possession.

But he and his people were undoubtedly the heirs and protectors, a right bequeathed to him by his forefathers. Sulayman stood evidence to that link as he was named after the very king rumored to have entrusted these objects to Sulayman's own ancestor for safekeeping. And, Sulayman displayed said king's great gift, even as much, because people would travel from afar to have Sulayman weigh in on a matter. This was how he came to his present situation.

He surveyed the scenes played out from his position on the hill outside his residence. Was he not king? Was it not his duty, religious or otherwise, to see this through? He was as conflicted as he was convicted. Surely, the revelation he'd just received (confirmed by a celestial occurrence that he, himself, had witnessed) would be occasion for great rejoicing if held true. The weight of it and what it could mean for him, for his subjects and their connection to the One True God's own people, fell on him.

Sulayman needed to verify the event for himself, with his own eyes. His heart quickened at the thought. Could it be true? At last? His consultation with an expert in the movement of the stars, a man whose opinion he truly respected, led Sulayman to hope, against hope, that it could be so. The mere thought made his heart ache to witness this great sight. That he could be fortunate enough to see the realization of this long anticipated event during his lifetime was *unfathomable*.

He gathered his thoughts and himself, turned away from his view and readied for the arduous, though joyful, journey ahead.

Chapter One

Martha

… lay awake, staring at the rough, thatched ceiling of her home. Moonlight peeked through the latticed window, taunting her. She felt it pressing on her eyelids but refused to open them and confront the offending glow. She tossed and turned, eyes closed, for some time before giving up. Sleep evaded her. It remained just out of her reach, testimony to her clamorous thoughts. Being home should have been easy, especially considering her recent absence when all she could do was wish for home, her mom, and a comfy pallet fortified with extra layers of goatskin between her and the packed dirt floor. Instead, the atmosphere was oppressive and dense around her. Even her thick braids seemed absurdly heavy.

"Puh!" She expelled a loud breath. Then she caught herself, sat up abruptly and looked around to see if she had awakened anyone. No need to have *two* sleepless people in the house. Actually, it would be rather more than two; she scanned the room for signs that her audible sigh had disturbed the rest of the sleepers. But they continued in peaceful slumber. She laid back, relieved and sighed again – this time through her nose, more quietly. She couldn't seem to help it. Martha had a lot on her mind.

Martha had a large family, made up of all sisters. Her father didn't mind, though. He adored his daughters. As he didn't have a male heir, his daughters could inherit his property due to an ancient and hardly utilized law. He saw to it that his girls understood this in case something should happen to him. He wanted them to know he had provided for them. He also, as much as he could, taught them regarding the sacred writings since his daughters were not allowed to receive formal instruction. That thought still rankled Martha.

Father had scholarly leanings and had passed his insatiable appetite for learning onto his children. Why should his daughters not learn the same as their male counterparts? Why should his children be denied education, simply because they were women? So he saw to the teaching of his household, on his own accord, including that of his wife. He often shared with them his views on politics and matters of law, as well as, the holy writings. Because of the allowances he made toward his daughters, he was frowned upon by his neighbors. Martha, they felt, was the most ruined of the lot. She smiled at the thought. Martha was his most apt pupil, she knew, for she took to learning voraciously. She had a thirst for knowledge that her father eagerly sated.

She didn't think Father had a favorite (and of course, he would deny it) but he did seem to be more partial towards her. Maybe that was because of her more independent attitude. He had no son, he may have reasoned. Why should his daughter not display the same forward thinking as himself? Or, perhaps, it was because she was the daughter who most resembled him, with her female version of his prominent nose. Martha loved her father, but how she hated that nose! Not on him, mind you – just on *her*.

She hoped that didn't make her a bad person. She wanted a dainty, pretty nose like her sisters, who had all inherited their mother's delicately flared nostrils. At least, Martha consoled herself, she had some compensating contributors to her appearance – eyes so dark that they appeared black and a glorious crown of curly, thick hair. Another sigh escaped at the vain path her musings had taken. The size of her nose was not why she couldn't sleep.

She had weightier concerns on her mind. But who among her family – mother, father, and sisters – could help her, even if they were awake? Who would understand what she'd been through? Where and *when* she'd been? A slight smile slanted her lips as she thought of her new friend, Ari, and Mal, more friend now than cousin. They alone knew. They would understand.

A baby wailed into the night, fretful. Martha wasn't the only one awake. She immediately searched the darkness for her youngest sibling and found her still and sound asleep in their father's arms. One tiny hand rested on his bearded cheek, and the other was entangled in his tunic. Her family slumbered on soundly, oblivious to the swelling cries of the child. Perplexed by the origin, she looked toward the moonbeams as if they could, somehow, help her discern the source of the sorrowful sounds. She thought of her friends and wondered if they, too, were unable to sleep.

Ari

... sat on his rooftop, gazing at the moon. The vegetation of the roof rustled underneath him as he shifted restlessly – signs that he and his uncles would soon have a project underway to create a new one. It was hot. Though, undoubtedly, the air would cool as the night progressed. For now, it was too warm for him to sleep indoors. Or perhaps it only felt so because he had slept outdoors more often than not recently. He felt stifled by the house this evening. But the night sky offered no consolation. The stars didn't seem to twinkle as brightly as they had when he was *elsewhere*, only a short time ago. In reality, it was far more than a few nights past. Generations had elapsed since that fateful battle in the Valley of *Elah*. And, they had met the Warrior King! Ari was truly in awe of the memory. Still, so many questions remained unanswered. He supposed the how of it didn't really matter to him as much as the *who*. Ari pulled his finely woven, linen mantle, upon which he'd been laying, close to his nose and breathed in deeply. He imagined that it held the hint of that *other* place, embedded deeply into the fabric now. Try as Ari might, he could not bring his thoughts under rein. Who was the Young Master that he could perform such deeds?

And, if they could go back in time, why couldn't he see his *patér* once again? Ari would give anything to see his father. Just one more time. It would be enough, he promised. It had to be.

"Ari?" His mother's hushed voice interrupted his thoughts. She was a light sleeper. "Can't you sleep, my *seh*?" The endearment, *my lamb*, rolled off him painlessly. This night, it didn't bother him nearly as much as it normally did. He had missed her so much that even babyish nicknames couldn't get a rise out of him. Mother had come soundlessly up the steps, but only partially so. She held a lamp aloft in her hand; her face was luminous in the soft glow.

14

His response was to slump his shoulders forward and rest his arms on his legs. Then, he ran his fingers through his hair and let his head fall into his hands before answering. He searched for words he could say to ease her. He didn't want her sleep to be disturbed, as was his own. Ari tried to hide his face, and thus his thoughts from his mom. She could be too discerning, at times.

"Thinking deep thoughts, *mētēr*," he whispered into the stillness, smiling at her in the darkness. "Just thinking deep thoughts."

His mother's laughter and affection were evident in her responding chuckle, albeit quietly. No need to raise her brothers and father from their slumber. Her son was the only remnant she had of her husband. Ari was a wonderful reminder, as he was the epitome of his father, but somehow a mixture of them both. His presence stood witness to their union. Ari looked back at her from calm gray eyes; a halo of frizzy, sandy blond hair framed his face. His coloring, which was so different from her own dark hair, eyes, and more pigmented skin, was inherited from her beloved.

"Well, try not to keep at it too late." She gave him a piercing look and tried not to let on that she knew something was bothering him. His hair gave it away. Normally curly, his hair now stuck out from his head at angles, indicating that he'd been doing a lot of "thinking" and pulling as he did so. But he wouldn't want her to worry. She knew he was grinning back at her, as only he could do now. So much like his father. "Get some sleep."

"I will," he promised. He could feel exhaustion creeping up on him and knew he wouldn't be awake much longer, despite his mental turmoil. His thoughts returned, unavoidably, to the Young Master. Rumors of healing and great miracles followed after that young prophet, creating more questions than answers. Ari had heard of them, pieces of conversation here and there, in only

16

the short time since they'd returned. It was all anyone could talk about. Incredibly, the blind were made to see again. Lame from birth were given to walk. Deaf ears were unstopped. And the dumb made to speak.

Ari laid back on the straw packed roof, feeling himself drift off with images of this same young prophet, the YM (for that is how he thought of the Young Master) foremost in his mind. *Who was He?*

Mal

… was restless. His first night back, and he still couldn't settle down. After putting Hannah to bed, he'd given up all pretense of sleep and laid on his back, staring at the rough ceiling. It had taken some time to console his little sister, but once he'd given her a story, as promised, all was forgiven. And who could blame her? His was a heroic tale, full of adventure and children with special talents. (He may, or may not, have let on that he and his friends were said children and Hannah may, or may not, have believed him.) His story had good characters, and evil beings bent on nefarious deeds. It held prophets, wondrous gifts, and even a giant! It was a fanciful story about events from a time long gone. And, it was true.

Mal kept touching familiar things to reassure himself that he was back home and not yet still in a time where King David was but a young man. It was not possible, but it was. It shouldn't have happened, and yet, it did. He shook his head and brought his meaty palms up, momentarily distracted by their size.

Gadol, he thought as he turned them over, staring at them. His limbs were big, just like the rest of him, and brown. He would never be considered fair skinned or gangly in build like his friend, Ari. Mal rubbed his face and pushed the heels of his hands into his eye sockets. But there was no way to un-see what he had witnessed. Yes, the events were real. Because of the Young Master, he and his friends were cast back in time to witness one of the greatest battles *ever*. They had even played their small part in preparing the young shepherd for the confrontation. And, David had called them his friends.

But how could they ever describe what had transpired? To whom had such things ever occurred, besides them? The event was too incredible to believe, and he daren't ask an adult to interpret. They would think him crazy or a liar. Mal supposed that Martha's summation made the most sense. She'd disclosed her theory on their walk home.

The closest approximation to explain the phenomenon would be something her father had once mentioned. *Laqach,* he had called it – as in when Enoch was taken away. Or maybe when the prophet Elijah was picked up in a fiery chariot to be seen by this world no more. But, these men had this in common; they did not return. They were never seen again. Mal, Ari, and Martha had come back. So was it the same? Mal didn't have an answer.

If that alone wasn't enough to keep him awake, they had somehow gained an enemy. A foe so evil, just the thought of him caused the hair on Mal's arms to stand on end. A terrible man, with the golden-green eyes of a predator, which shone out from inhumanly beautiful features. And don't forget the serpent-like tongue, Mal reminded himself, shuddering at the memory. Now this *strange man* was after Mal and his friends.

He rose from his pallet and let himself out of the house, taking a moment to scan over his sleeping family before he stepped into the moonlight. Mother and Hannah slept in each other's arms, bronze limbs entangled, while Abigail held her place, which was furthest from the door. He gazed upon their peaceful features with a trace of envy. How could he be expected to sleep with so much information to

20

absorb? He was consumed by his thoughts; were they (he, Ari, and Martha) too hasty in their assent?

"Even knowing all that you know now," the Young Master had queried, "would you still say yes?"

And he, Martha and Ari had all been in agreement, rather too quickly, perhaps. But there was too much they didn't know about their gifts, their responsibilities, and their mission. Too many unknowns, he thought, though he didn't want to recant. To go back to what he was, to say no to the Young Master would be to lose his gift. The thought was unimaginable. He experienced a heady rush, just at the possibility of using his power again and couldn't resist its pull. Mal raised his right hand and drew in the night sky with his finger, willing the air to follow the pattern.

"*YES*," he'd written. And to his astonishment, the letters hung there, a declaration of some sort, solidifying his earlier allegiance to the young prophet.

Yes, again he thought, nodding to himself in the darkness. All Mal could think was, he didn't want to go back. There was no way he would give up his gift. He didn't want to be the same. He didn't want to live *un*changed. He felt a bit torn over the decision, knowing it was somewhat selfish to want the gift only because he felt powerful. It seemed ... *irresponsible*.

Take care of your sisters, his mother urged often. So he did. And Father entrusted Mal to do the same for Mother. *Watch over your Ima.* Father's parting words were always directed towards Mal. As a fisherman, Father was gone more often than not. It was a hard living and kept Father away from family for extended periods. So Mal's whole life had been imbued with a sense of duty – to his father, mother, and sisters. His urge to be responsible was completely at odds with his current train of thought. It felt *different* to want something just for himself.

Mal wandered down to the beach by a path he could have walked even in darkest night and found one of his favorite places to play when he was a small child. Cool, wet sand muffled his footsteps as he approached the old boat, no longer suitable for fishing and partially buried in the ground. The protruding bow still had just enough room for Mal, and he lowered his hulking form down into it. The boat was smaller than he remembered (either that or more of it had become covered over time) for he barely had room to maneuver. Mal settled in as best he could, and cast his gaze out over the calm sea with the moon shimmering on its surface, and wished he felt the same. He lay snug, cradled within the tight confines of the dinghy, recalling some of the last words of the Young Master and peace came over him. Mal grew drowsy as that conversation with the prophet replayed in his mind, providing comfort and a soothing balm for his troubled thoughts.

"Don't worry. I have good plans for you – have courage and have faith!"

Chapter Two

Mal slept fitfully, despite his remembrance of the Young Master's encouraging words. A woman was crying. A woman with a baby. No – babies? Women clutching lifeless babes to their breasts. Screams. Terror! He had to help her – *them*. Death! Despair! He must protect! Defend! Avenge! He awakened with a start – fearful, chest heaving, heart thudding – to find Ari and Martha standing over him. Groggy and disoriented from the dream, he was less than well-mannered.

"What? Wha- what?" He looked around quickly, trying to get his bearings. Where was he? On the beach, he realized when his hand touched sand as he nearly rocked himself out of the wrecked vessel. He couldn't have slept long for it was still dark. Dawn was yet hours away. Bleary eyed and disgruntled, the cries of women and babes echoed in his head, further addling his brain. "Did you wake me? Why? Why are you here?" He gasped as the rapidly cooling night air permeated his throat and expanded his lungs.

"We had problems sleeping," Ari answered for himself and Martha. "Same as you, by the looks of it," he added dryly. Judging by their demeanor, Mal knew that their restlessness was only a portion of his. Ari and Martha had happened upon Mal as he struggled in his sleep and heard him cry out. Mal's tunic clung to him in a way that indicated he'd been sweating and not just from the prior day's heat. Beads of perspiration were gathered on his forehead and upper lip.

"And, we were drawn here," Martha piped in. An irresistible pull was more like it. "Well, Ari saw me leaving my home from his rooftop and decided to follow." She stooped and touched her cousin's forehead, her own brow marred by a frown. "Mal, are you well?" Motherly concern etched her features and tinged her speech.

"Girls have no business wandering off by themselves in the middle of the night," Ari asserted, the protector in him riled.

"I was perfectly safe," Martha countered scathingly. "I've lived here my whole life! I would have been fine without you following me."

"It is not good for you to be alone," Ari insisted.

"I can protect myself better than either of you," Martha fumed. Sparks flew from her fingers, and she formed a ball of fire in her hand at will, knowing it was unwarranted as she was in no danger. But she wanted to remind him of just *who* had activated their gift first.

"Oh, really?" Ari cast a glance over his shoulder at the vast body of water. Plenty of liquid to douse her fireball. As he prepared to do just that, Mal intervened.

"Ari was right to follow you," Mal broke in sleepily, his stretch from his position on the rocky sand was punctuated by a great yawn, thus ending, he hoped, an argument he suspected they'd had the whole way. "You shouldn't be out alone at night, Martha." She left it at that, deferring to her older cousin but made a face at Ari. He was gracious in his victory; instead of further berating her, Ari chose to change the subject.

"Who could sleep with all that wailing anyway?" Ari cut in, eager to extend the olive branch to Martha, and not wanting her to remain angry with him. Besides that, whining little ones, in general, were not on his list of favorite people. *Enough racket to wake the dead*, his father used to say. Ari could put up with it when necessary. But he'd rather not.

"You heard it, too?" Mal shot up, suddenly more alert. All vestiges of sleep fell from his eyes. Ari and Martha looked puzzled as they glanced at each other and shrugged. "You heard the cries of the babies – of their mothers?" His voice cracked. The tumult haunted him, still, rending his heart.

"One cry. One baby. Not plural," Ari answered cheekily, emphasizing the "one" in both statements by raising his index finger. Mal had to be exaggerating though Ari tended to agree with his friend. That baby created enough of a ruckus for twins. He shook his head at his friend but quickly sobered when he saw that Mal was serious. Whatever he'd heard had disturbed him greatly.

"No – I heard many babies – so many babies … and their mothers …" He pressed his fingers into his eye sockets, seeking relief from the sickening images the voices conjured. Or could he see them? He couldn't tell the dream from reality anymore. The wails of the children haunted him still, murmuring and continuing in a low drone as he spoke, so much that he questioned whether he was awake or yet in his dream.

Martha and Ari were talking to him – he could see their lips moving, soundlessly. They both seemed quite normal, aside from the way they were looking at him. Couldn't they hear it? The cries and shouts were increasing in volume. Confusion and pain lit his face, along with a look of such misery that his companions reached for him, to comfort him. Just at that moment, a piercing scream broke through the cacophony. Mal grabbed his head in agony, rolled over and out of the little boat altogether. He curled into a fetal position as the deafening concert of voices broke through his consciousness and overwhelmed him, threatening to swallow him whole. Martha fell to her knees and grabbed her cousin as he convulsed while Ari caught Mal's head just before it slammed a rock. And that was all it took. The pain and the voices immediately stopped. But Ari, Mal, and Martha were gone.

But why was he afraid? Better yet, why were Ari, Mal, and Martha here? They knew what had happened, just not why. The YM's gifts had called them here, to this place, for a reason. They all wondered why they were witness to this display, the cowing of one person by another being of (they supposed) greater significance. From the sumptuous display of wealth, they gathered they'd been sent someplace important. Golden urns were placed at intervals; their dark paintings featured men armed with bow or sword and riding in chariots. One even depicted a half man, half beast, playing a lute. The ornately decorated vessels were in various sizes, for varied purposes (they assumed, as someone was retching into one just then) and were strategically placed all about the ... palace?

That was it! It dawned on them then that this must be the home of a high dignitary – maybe even a king. The intricate scrolls and carvings on the column appeared to be of Roman origin, Ari noted.

Again, their eyes were drawn upward to victorious battle scenes displayed in stark relief upon the frieze that ran along the border of the ceiling. An "Oh!" almost escaped Martha as she gazed in wonder. Ari held a warning finger to his lips. The voices carried on as the children continued to take in their surroundings:

"Certainly! Yes, certainly, once you have found what you seek, you MUST come back!" Again, with the emphasis, even more so on that word. And it was spoken with great authority as if the one who spake were used to his every command being obeyed. He said *must* as if there were no choice in the matter but not in a threatening manner. The speaker sounded quite happy and overly jovial. "Yes! Yes!" Each *yes* was accompanied by the maniacal sounds of clapping hands. "You *must* come back after your travels so that I, too, may join in the celebration!" His voice oozed false sincerity. Mal bugged his eyes in disbelief. Ari's raised eyebrow and Martha's slowly shaking head clearly agreed with Mal's assessment. They crept forward, drawn by the voice and its high pitched, disingenuous tone. The children stole a look around the stone cylinder.

Four men stood before a dais, their elaborately covered heads bowed, where a man sat on a throne. His crown of beaten gold glittered with jewels and sat slightly askew above a face flushed, quite possibly, from too much wine. He was dressed according to the Roman fashion, Ari noticed. The crown bearer wore a light tunic of the finest linen with a strip of purple bordering the edges as adornment. The woolen fabric of his toga was of the same deep hue and draped about his person. It was gathered to one shoulder and held with a golden clasp. A cup dangled from his finger. It must have been empty for he called for more drink. For the first time, the children noticed that his speech slurred. He was definitely under the influence of his alcoholic beverage. The group of men before him seemed subdued and receptive in the face of his insistence. That was, perhaps, because he was a king. But at least two of the men at the foot of his throne appeared, themselves, to be royalty.

The four were dressed in lordly fashion; rich, colorful robes adorned them, made of fabrics and shades the children had seldom seen. Obviously, the men had dressed for an audience with the king. Surely, the cloth alone must have cost a fortune. All the men bore head coverings of some sort. Until that moment, as the children cast their gaze about, their surroundings had a somewhat familiar look to it – from the palatial residence to its accoutrements. There was this vague sense that they knew something about this place. These men, however, were out of place, foreign and exotic.

One, by the look of him, was clearly Egyptian. He stood out because of his height. Towering over his companions, he bore a wig of straight locks (impossibly so) upon his head from which wooden beads dangled and shook whenever he moved. The robe hung uncomfortably off his shoulder and was a little too short for the tunic he wore underneath as if it were borrowed. The children could see (from their vantage point) the kohl outline of his eyes extending to the side of his face. That was the most the children could make of the facial features of the group.

Another stood out because he was the widest of the group though he had height to match. It was hard to gauge from his backside, whether his width was because he was rotund or just that big. His clothing rivaled that of the ruler who sat upon the throne. The large man had a silk tunic that peeked underneath his rich robing. A turban of vibrant color sat upon his head, indicating that this big, wide fellow, too, was royalty. The third man had a riot of wavy hair - dense, shiny and dark - which his own head wrap could hardly contain. The hands clasped behind his back were the color of cinnamon, and his fingers were covered in bejeweled rings. The final fellow had a cap of closely cropped hair. He was sweating profusely and kept mopping his brow with the end of his head covering, which was coming undone. He slung the tail of it over his shoulder and about his neck, cowl-like. He was the smallest of the lot.

But, the being that garnered the most attention, heretofore unnoticed, was the one who stood next to the king, at his very elbow. He hung like an appendage on the king's ear, whispering words as the king parroted:

"You must *certainly* come back and give a full report of your findings," the king said again, full of high spirits.

To a casual observer, it might appear the king was babbling. But babbling has no direction. This message was specifically pointed in one direction. It said: *come back* almost as if by saying it repeatedly, he could program the action into the hearers. As the children stood watching, the eyes of the ruler gleamed darkly in the flickering torchlight, then suddenly flashed full of radiance so quickly that the children thought they might have imagined it. Just then, the head that was bent toward the king, and to which the king paid such rapt attention, lifted and was suddenly illuminated. All three children inhaled sharply as his visage was displayed. A perfect smile parted to reveal a flickering tongue set in an inhumanly beautiful face. Golden-green eyes returned their gaze. Ari, Mal, and Martha were looking directly into the face of the Strange Man.

Chapter Four

They had last seen the Strange Man at the battle between David (their friend and Warrior King) and Goliath, the giant defeated in the Valley of *Elah*. Martha shut her eyes tightly and prayed that he did not see them. This tactic had worked once before, creating a fog so dense that it was impenetrable to the naked eye. But alas, no such cloud cover came to her rescue this time. He saw them, to her dismay. The Strange Man filled her with such disquiet that she had hoped never to see him again. He smiled at her in sinister fashion, his eyes flashing golden-green as he met her own.

Unlike Martha, Ari, and Mal, the Strange Man did not seem surprised or overly perturbed at their appearance. He seemed quite pleased with himself, actually smirking at them while he spoke into the king's ear. Could it be that whatever good work they had been sent to achieve had already been circumvented by the presence of such malevolence?

The king carried on in a loud, increasingly domineering tone. They realized now that the king was being influenced by more than just alcohol. The Strange Man manipulated the king like a puppet on a string.

"You must, you must, you must," he insisted, in that now familiar cadence, first slow, then faster, growing more insistent. The king's eyes flashed again, and the children knew then that this was not their imagination. The Strange Man bent to the king's ear once more, his tongue flickering while he spoke. His mouth uttered words they knew would soon be heard from the king's own lips. The leonine eyes of the Strange Man glittered and never left them. He wanted them to see the control he had over the king, whose own eyes now flashed in synchronization with the Strange Man's. When the king did speak again, it was in a voice they did not recognize, full of power and crushing in its insistence.

41

"You WILL, won't you? *You will report to me*," a statement more than a question, followed by a very clear command. The smallest of the men, bobbed his head up and down, responding to the direct order in the voice of the king.

"Yes, sire," came the quick reply, with more up and down of the head. "Of course. We are *sure* to return." But Martha could hear the "no" in the little man's voice, even as he nodded his head. The king, however, seemed oblivious and beamed at the group in a satisfied way. He wasn't concerned with the truth of the statement, apparently, only that he had their pledge to return. This appeared to satisfy the Strange Man, too, for he straightened at that and smiled his beautiful smile directly at Martha and her group, meeting their eyes. His expression was smug as if he knew he'd thwarted them.

But how? Had he indeed won a game they didn't even know about, nor did they understand the stakes? No answers were forthcoming as the

Strange Man suddenly departed, leaving the king's side and sauntering through the group of men. As in the valley of *Elah*, the men parted like water before the Strange Man, but otherwise, didn't appear to notice him. Their bodies moved, unconsciously, to avoid that which didn't even register. It seemed he was invisible to all but the interloping youngsters.

The next moment he was before the children, in the blink of an eye. They gasped and withdrew in the face of their foe, not expecting such a confrontation. He veered close enough for the trio to see his glowing cat-like orbs flare up and flash golden-green again. And then he was gone, with naught but his laughter to mock them long after.

****

Puzzled, the children clung to the shadowy recess and traded whispers:

"What was that about?" Martha held her hand to her chest in an attempt to calm the inhabitant of that cavity. Her heart was thumping so hard from the fright; she feared it might come clean out of her body.

"I have no idea," Ari remarked as if he were not ruffled by the whole exchange. But he was likewise unnerved by the encounter.

"Whatever it is," Mal warned grimly, "it can't be good."

The king's head snapped up as if awakening from a trance. He viewed the group of men before him, unable to recall what he had been doing the moment before. Ah, yes! He remembered. The child.

"You may go," he dismissed, with a regal flick of his wrist. On an afterthought, he leaned towards the men and gave them a hard look through narrowed eyes. "But remember your pledge."

With bowed heads, the group of men retreated, backing away. The eyes of the children watched as the men exited the room, and they assumed, the palace. Ari bugged his eyes, motioning after the men excitedly, *follow them.* They scurried along, hugging the walls and trying to find the way out without being seen. The children managed to catch sight of one colorful robe and hurried to catch up. Mal drew up sharply at the sound of footfalls. Ari and Martha nearly bowled him over when he came to a sudden stop. They heard it, too. Sandaled feet were coming swiftly in their direction, but came to a halt just before uncovering the children in their hiding place. The trio held their breath, afraid that any sound could lead to their discovery. Voices.

"Stay with them. Understand?" This was said in a curt tone which held little tolerance for debate. "Find out where they're staying. Learn what you can about where they're going. On the king's orders," he finished the command. Mal peeked from their hiding place. Ari risked a glance over Mal's shoulder. Martha did the same, down below his knee. By their armor, Ari recognized them as Roman soldiers. One nodded while the other spoke, and the children quickly shied back to avoid being seen. Soon they heard the slapping sounds of sandal-shod feet, those of the soldier carrying out orders as he was bidden.

"And try not to be obvious," the commanding officer called after the retreating footfalls.

Chapter Five

All of a sudden, it came to Ari where he had seen this place, but there was no time to explain. Putting his finger to his lips, he indicated with widened eyes, lifted brows and a jerk of his head over his shoulder that his companions should follow him. He would fill them in later. His friends followed his lead unquestioningly, figuring he knew something they did not know. Instinctively, he led them through the corridors, knowing which rooms to avoid and where they would be least likely to encounter the inhabitants of the residence. Finally, he turned a corner that led to an unattended door. Yes, Ari thought, just as he'd remembered.

The trio snuck out of the palace without further incident and hid in a patch of tall grass. Once outside, they took in their surroundings. It was night here, too. More Roman soldiers patrolled the outskirts of the huge establishment (now that they were outside, they had some idea of just how large a building) and its grounds. Some soldiers were on foot, others on horseback. The scene looked too familiar: the men, buckled into their armor, the opulence of the palatial grounds glistening in the moonlight. Could it be that they were in their own time, still?

Just then, the children caught sight of the four men who'd met previously with the king as they were leaving. The four noblemen paused suddenly under a torch and huddled together, their colorful robes catching the light. The young soldier (who had been dispatched to follow them), melted into the darkness when the group before him halted.

"Get down!" Ari hissed at Mal and Martha. Too curious, their heads had ventured up above the tall grass so that they could see better. They all ducked their heads and pressed themselves close to the ground.

"Why?" Mal whispered back furiously, his eyebrows drawn together. Martha looked around anxiously for signs that someone had seen them.

Ari lowered his voice, "I just don't think it's a good idea to be seen by soldiers. How would we explain our presence *here*?" Martha nodded in agreement. That made sense. Then, another thought occurred to her.

"Wait – I know where we are." It dawned on Martha as she viewed the portico; she *had* seen this building before, on their many excursions with their families on holy days. This was the City of David, the home of THE king, their present day king (or not, as her father would have it). They were in *Yerushalaim*. And Ari must have known the layout because he'd been here many times with his father.

"I recognize this place –" All conversation was cut off as Martha was snatched up in the air, her legs windmilling furiously as she tried to escape the clutches of a leering soldier. In her eagerness to tell Mal and Ari what she'd discerned, she'd unwittingly revealed their location.

Mal and Ari jumped up to defend her and were caught, too, before they could put up much of a fuss. Mal's arms were pinned behind his head as he struggled to gain freedom. Ari's hands were captured behind his back, and after initially resisting, he made himself speak calmly:

"Let. Her. Go." He tried to retain his composure outwardly, but inwardly he was seething over their treatment, especially of Martha. Still, he wanted to avoid further confrontation, so he forced himself to maintain a level voice. "Put her down, *now*."

"Ah – look at the young pup! Thinks he can order us around, does he?" And all of the soldiers laughed at this, the idea of a boy giving them orders. Meanwhile, Martha's foot landed in an unguarded spot, bringing an "oomph!" and low muttered curse from the soldier. Before he could react, Ari interjected.

"I must insist that you cease your treatment of us, or I shall be forced to appeal to Caesar!" His voice rose at the last, trying to infuse every bit of threat that he could muster into the title of the genuine sovereign of the entire region.

"Oh! Now he knows *Caesar*, does he?" The soldier repeated, causing another round of laughter. The disbelief was plain on his face.

"I am a Roman citizen," Ari asserted. He looked the soldier straight in the eye as he said it and drew himself up as tall as his confinement would allow. "It is my right to appeal to him."

This made the young soldier pause. He gave Ari a measuring look, trying to gauge whether his claim was truthful. The youth did not wear a *toga*, the expected garb of a free Roman citizen. Still, there was a look about the boy. The soldier noted the carriage of the young man and the high quality of his tunic. Could be the lad spoke the truth. The beefy infantryman (Ari could tell the fellow was of low rank) set Martha down on her feet, slowly. Mal's arms were released; he flexed his arms, rolling his shoulders as he turned to glare at his jailer. Ari just as suddenly found his hands were free.

"Well, you didn't have to carry on so," the brutish soldier insisted. "Just having a bit of fun with ya – no harm done, right?" He lifted his head at Ari, daring him to say otherwise. After another tense moment, Ari gave a curt nod in response.

Roman citizenship could be bought if you had enough money or earned through military service, as in the case of the soldier. So how was it that this young boy had already attained the status of citizen? He asked it of Ari.

"I was born a citizen. My father, my *patér*, is–
" he stammered but finished strongly, "a
Centurion." *Was*, he mentally corrected but found
himself unable to give voice to that truth. His father
was no longer.

"Yea?" The soldier became more animated,
less surly at that revelation. "Maybe I know of him."
Highborn, highbred, with enough wealth to buy
status, he may not know. But he definitely
understood and knew about fellow soldiers. He felt
more warmly towards Ari and his companions at
this bit of information.

Ari, too, was feeling more inclined to be
forgiving of their mistreatment at the thought. This
man may have known his father! Just as he opened
his mouth to give his father's name, they were
interrupted.

"Enough racket going on over here to wake
the dead!" Ari whirled in surprise at the familiar

phrase and the voice he would never forget. His eyes searched the night anxiously, desperately, seeking confirmation. He held his breath at the approach of a soldier, walking towards them with a familiar, jaunty stride. Ari knew it as well as his own. Armor gleaming in the moonlight, the man removed his plumed helmet and tucked it under his arm as he came, but his face remained hidden. The newcomer stepped out of the shadow until he was illuminated by the torchlight. And Ari gasped as he looked directly into the face of his dad.

Chapter Six

Mal and Martha stared at the man before them, knowing undoubtedly Ari's parentage. Ari's father wore the typical uniform of the Roman soldier of their time: breastplate, metal hinged jacket overlaying a woolen tunic, leather apron to gird his lower body and greaves to cover his shins. Even his armor could not conceal the lean, muscular physique underneath, in contrast to the stout and squat appearance of Erasmus. It was betrayed in the ripples of movement along his exposed arms and legs. And it was in his bearing. He stood tall, proud and erect – a clear foreshadow of the man Ari would become.

The resemblance was eerie. Nearly Ari's duplicate, he appeared to be at ease, and his face was creased in a jovial manner. But his right hand rested on his hip near the short sword he carried, belying his easy going demeanor and readying himself for any situation that should arise. Martha's eyes roamed back and forth between them, comparing their features. *It couldn't be*, she thought. Mal was flat-out flummoxed. Speechless. Bug-eyed. Just what was going on here?

"Pa- ... h-how ... w-wha-" Ari was frozen to the spot, his mouth opening and closing like a fish while he struggled to piece his thoughts together. The face that he never expected to see again swam before his vision and tears misted his eyes. He blinked to clear them. This wasn't real. His *patér* was dead. He knew this. Yet, here his father stood before him and very much alive. Ari continued to gape in astonishment, then gave up all pretense of trying to speak and flung himself at his father.

"Hold – whoa, whoa, there!" The newcomer rocked back on his heels at the impact and set Ari back on his own feet, not ungently. "Boy – what ails you?" The soldier looked around helplessly at the group before him, but his comrades looked similarly puzzled. When he attempted to turn Ari's face up to meet him, Ari clung to him all the more. That is, before Ari was peeled, quite forcefully, off of his father's trim and uniformed figure.

"I'm thinking you lied to us, young pup," the big soldier said menacingly while leaning in to get in Ari's face. "You said your father was a centurion. Even if this were him, he ain't no commanding officer. Eh, Jules?" And he shook Ari a little, at every other word, outraged that he had fallen for such a ploy.

Jules (that is, Ari's father, Julius) held out his hand to halt what was surely a blow aimed at Ari's head. The massive palm would've undoubtedly done some damage. "Leave him be, Erasmus. He's just a kid – not worth getting worked up about." Sneering at Jules' assessment of the situation, Erasmus grudgingly released Ari. Jules took Ari by the arm and pulled Ari to his side. He effectively put himself between Erasmus and the boy, thwarting any further actions by the disgruntled soldier. "If it'll make you feel any better, he's mine. I'm claiming him – I'll take responsibility for him and his friends." He smiled at each of them, one at a time.

Erasmus considered the proposition before him and his options. He really didn't want to fight Julius for the right to punish the boy. Erasmus was more wide than tall. His pushed in face was evidence of many brawls with him being on the receiving end of a good punch. Though Julius was leaner and slighter in appearance than himself, Erasmus was not fooled; Julius was a born fighter and fierce besides. It would not be an easy fight. An ugly win at best. Besides that, Julius was, technically, his superior, even if only in their tent.

In the end, Erasmus dropped his guard and relaxed his stance. He hulked away, shooting backward glances in their direction, his eyes warning retribution if the opportunity ever arose. The children breathed a collective sigh of relief when he entered a tent and was out of their eyesight, taking his companions with him.

"I could hardly leave you with him. Erasmus can be a good enough fellow, just not quite right in the head sometimes." Julius tapped his temple by way of explanation. As he did, he looked them over with a confused expression. His gaze lit on Ari. "What is this all about? Am I supposed to know you?"

Mal and Martha took in the scene and knew immediately that they were seeing double. The two were unmistakably identical, except for size and coloring. Whereas Ari's light complexion was more brown than red, and his hair texture was more wiry and curly in comparison to Julius', the features (and expressions) were the same, right down to the gray eyes. Though, admittedly, Ari's eyes were a tad grayer whilst Jules' irises held a hint of blue.

"*Should* I know you?" he asked again, more perplexed than ever. Still no response from Ari, who had finally noticed something was off. Thinking that something was *not quite right* with Ari and his companions either, Jules tried a different approach. "What is your name, son?"

"I am called Ari," he managed, at last. Ari looked about him, looking for more clues as to where they were. And when. Perhaps he had it all wrong. Maybe this Julius was not his father, the Roman centurion. Details, details, Ari thought fleetingly, searching his fuzzy memories for more information. What was different? But Jules had to be his father, he argued with himself. Jules looked just like his father, with the same name. What were the odds? Not to mention, he was a soldier, though apparently, not an officer. Ari realized that Julius was speaking.

"Ari," he repeated, testing the name and deciding he liked the sound of it. "As in

Aristophanes? That's a fine, strong name," Jules chuckled as he, too, noted their resemblance. "And it appears to be one befitting a handsome youngster as yourself." Ari took that last comment for what it was, a reference to his own name, which actually meant *best appearing* and a compliment to the speaker himself. Jules winked at the young man before him and leaned in, conspiratorially, before adding, "I imagine that if I *did* have a son one day, I'd like to call him the same." He sought to bring comfort to the boy. Evidently, Ari was reminded of someone very dear to him. But, it wasn't Jules. He was sure he'd never met the lad. Still, Ari stared at Jules like one who'd come back from the dead.

Ari searched Jules' features for some clues that he was mistaken. He compared the distant memories of his *patér* to the man before him, taking notice of the lack of gray hair in Jules hairline. Ari also noted the slighter figure of this man as he spoke. Where was his paunch – the one that his father so fondly patted and was lovingly teased about? Admittedly, it wasn't much of a protrusion, but father used to always go on about how it had gotten bigger since the days of his youth.

THAT WAS IT! Ari almost snapped his fingers and slapped his forehead in relief. He wasn't deranged. The voices of his friends broke through his consciousness. Mal and Martha introduced themselves and apologized for his behavior while he stared off into space.

"Right," he came back to himself dazedly. "I do apologize. I thought you were someone else. It was a … a shock, like I was seeing a ghost." His own father didn't know him. He let that bit of news settle on him. Suddenly morose, he blinked back tears. Julius looked horrified at the boy's display of emotion and thought: what could be so wrong to make this man-child cry? But before he could inquire further, a disturbance broke out nearby and claimed his attention.

"I'll be right back," he called over his shoulder as he jogged to the source of the commotion. Obviously, one of his duties (assigned or assumed) was keeping the peace within their unit. Beyond him, the eyes of the children were drawn to the steps of the palace. A figure loitered in the courtyard. Even under cover of darkness, the children knew him. His form was becoming all too familiar. He lifted his head, and the light from the torches revealed his uncommonly beautiful features and confirmed their suspicions. He gave his perfect smile. They could just make out the snakelike tongue that flickered about his lips in mockery of a normal man. But this was not a mere man.

Chapter Seven

The children stepped back at the sight, seeking the darkness. They concealed themselves in the overgrown vegetation that bordered the Roman garrison. Seeing the Strange Man again was not good news, but it wasn't a surprise considering the present goings on. The dissension among the unit increased with his appearance, on par with what the Young Master had told them:

"Where there is unrest, confusion, dissension, and any sort of evil work afoot, you will find him."

But why was he still here? For that matter, why were they? And what did Ari's father have to do with any of this? Whatever the reason for the presence of the Strange Man, they could be assured that he was up to no good. The ruckus increased as the Strange Man came to the forefront, no longer hidden in shadow and divided their attention. He raised one arm and, while holding his hand aloft, pointed at the disturbance and made a little twisting motion with his hand as if he were turning a dial.

The children recognized the young soldier who was assigned to follow the four men in the midst of the disturbance. Alópéx, as he was called, was a thin fellow given to scurrying along quite quickly. Sly as the fox, from which he'd derived his nickname, it was in his skill set to trail a person, undetected. The Fox was also easily excitable. After losing sight of his quarry, he'd returned, empty handed. And he was in trouble because of his slack. Incensed, the commanding officer (easily identifiable to Ari by his transversely plumed helmet and his short sword on the left side), boxed his ears and hurled insults at the offender, saying he would bring trouble on all their heads.

The young soldier, however, was unrepentant, even as he held his bleeding ear. It was hardly his fault that they seemed to disappear into a wall of fog so dense that he couldn't even see where he was walking. He was forced to abandon his mission, for fear of what hole he could stumble upon and do damage to himself. Indeed, his lower legs bore the evidence of his determination to follow the men, despite being, to all intents and purposes, blind. The soldier was eventually expelled from the cloud, quite forcibly. Otherwise, he could not have been so easily deterred. Since his commander was already infuriated, Alópéx thought it best not even to mention that the cloud spat him out. The men he pursued, in the Fox's estimation, were either lost in this same fog and had come to their doom, or had simply disappeared. This started another argument.

"How could FOUR MEN simply disappear?" The officer raged at the soldier. Then as quickly as tempers flared, they suddenly died down. The commanding officer assumed control, instead of arguing back against insubordination. He had the younger soldier taken into custody to await his fate.

The young soldier, for his part, seemed subdued and quiet, no longer defiant.

The Strange Man was gone now. Apparently, he'd taken off while the children were looking at the squabble. Had he seen them? Where did he go? Of a surety, they would not go looking for him. They had a feeling this would not be the last time they saw him.

"Er, kids? Children?" Julius was calling, his eyes owlishly boring into the night, looking for them. He whispered emphatically, "Ari!" But instead of coming forward, Ari stepped back further, trying to lose himself in the tall grass. His friends followed suit. Julius tried again, "Martha ... Mal ..." Still no answer. With a shake of his head, he gave up and rejoined his fellow soldiers.

Ari and his friends held their breath for a long time after he had left. Mal and Martha weren't sure why Ari would avoid his father, given a second chance to see him. But Ari couldn't face a father right now that didn't know him. It pained as much as it pleased.

****

After they had left Julius and the fort far behind (Ari led the way, for he seemed most familiar with the area), the children stepped out of the shadows. They didn't mean to, actually, but it was unavoidable as the night seemed especially bright. They clung to what they could of the darkness, walking until the vegetation gave way to a well-trodden path. You couldn't call it a road, really, for it was unpaved. Just a route that the local people commonly took that became worn over time. The troika set out on it, hoping it would lead to a nearby home and sustenance. The Young Master had sent them here; perhaps he had also provided someone to care for them. Finally, after putting some distance between themselves, the palace and the guards, they were able to speak about what had happened.

"Uhm ..." Mal began, "That *was* your father, right?" Even though he felt he knew the answer, he was puzzled that Ari would walk away from an opportunity to be with his father again. Other than a curt nod, no other answer was forthcoming.

"I can see how it would be hard to see him now," Martha blurted into the silence abruptly. Ari's head swiveled in her direction. She understood? How? He didn't yet understand it himself.

"It's like when my *savta* looks at me sometimes but doesn't know me," she continued. "I have all these memories of things we've done together, but she doesn't. At times, she thinks I'm my mother as a young girl, so she talks to me like I'm her little daughter." Martha rambled on. "There are so many things I want to tell her or even ask her about, but when she gets like that, she doesn't have the slightest recollection of me. She looks right through me." She stopped her musing to look kindly at Ari. "What I don't understand is why. Why doesn't he know you, Ari?"

Ari's head bobbed up and down in agreement. She did get it. "Because," Ari expelled a breath on a big sigh and answered despondently, "I haven't been born yet."

Chapter Eight

Ari explained his theory – the Julius that they'd just met was a younger version of his father before he had become a centurion. Prior, even, to having either wife or child – that's why he didn't recognize his own son.

"What? But that is incredible!" Mal exclaimed in disbelief. Not to mention, it was a little unfair. To see your recently deceased father and not have him know you was just ... unfair. No other word would suffice.

In a detached way, Martha had pulled all of the facts together, disseminated them, and made them make sense. But she was far from unaffected. Her heart went out to Ari.

"But this is not right," she objected strenuously. She sought for more forceful words, but none came to mind. Silently, Ari agreed with them both but was at a loss, too, for more words. It was actually too painful to see his father like this. This man was not yet his beloved *patér*.

Unbelievable that his father could see him but wouldn't know him. Unbelievable, that Ari would see the sight that he longed for, prayed to see ever since his father had passed. But more unbelievable than their own ability to move in and out of time? No. He slumped along dejectedly, as did the others, in complete sympathy with their friend. Indeed, Ari didn't know how to feel. Even though Jules didn't know him (yet), Ari had gotten what he'd wanted – to see his father again – right? He should be grateful, he knew. Still, it was so unfair. The Young Master, he was responsible for this. On this point, they all agreed.

So caught up were they in their musing that it took some time to realize the night was no longer clear. A low fog had risen from the ground. It crept slowly toward them and increased in height as it approached.

"Wha–" Ari cried as the dense cloud enveloped his feet. And suddenly, he couldn't see his hand before his face. He came to a halt altogether and put his hands before him, feeling altogether blind. Now they knew what had happened to the young soldier. A small hand found his, grasped and squeezed it, reassuringly.

"Don't worry," Martha said. "It's like mine." It certainly felt like her talent, although she didn't call for it. This cloud inspired the same feelings of comfort and safety within her. It felt familiar, like home. And she knew as long as she was encapsulated within, danger could not reach her there. She trusted the cloud, even though she didn't know why her gift had come to her aid. She reached for Mal, too, feeling along his arm until his big hand wrapped around hers. She found that the fog actually propelled them forward – its urge was irresistible. She held onto her friends and gave in to its direction, letting the cloud lead where it would.

They were getting closer to muffled voices, raised animatedly. And light – the light of a campfire, though small. The fog lifted, leaving them near the end of an overgrown path. The moon was bright overhead, once again, lighting their way. The children veered off the path and followed the sounds, through tall grass and small trees, curious as to what had the speakers so worked up. They moved silently. Well, as quietly as they could. Ari would turn to glare at Mal whenever he felt the bigger boy was being especially heavy footed. Stealthy, Big Mal was not.

As they drew near to a clearing, they didn't recognize the voices, but the shapes surrounding the fire looked vaguely familiar. They came nigh to the figures, not sure if they should run from the scene or ask for sustenance. Hunger won out, for they found they were altogether famished. The aroma of food drifted towards them, and it occurred to them (Ari, especially) that they could pilfer a bit while the strangers were otherwise engaged. Surely, there would be no harm. Appetite overrode reason.

Bits and pieces of the conversation filtered through their consciousness as they pondered their chances of success. When they drew closer to the men, the children could hear more clearly.

"Yes – but we gave our word," insisted one voice, high pitched and near hysteria. "It may cost our lives if we are caught!"

"No, we can't go back there," said another. "We have seen it in the stars. This man will do a great evil if we reveal the location."

"He will, no matter what we do," reasoned another low voice, not as distraught as the others. He seemed resigned. "This has already been set in motion by events beyond our control. It cannot be stopped now. The least we can do is not to give aid to evil."

"But the prophecy–"

"I have no care for your prophecy – you weary me with its very mention," an impatient voice interjected. "As to your promise, it occurs to me that he sought to bind you with your word because he perceived *you* were honorable men. He, himself, is not. Mark my speech – you can't trust anything he says. I've seen his type before. Going back will only bring trouble on all our heads," the voice continued, taking on a bragging tone.

"What he didn't count on was one, such as myself, full of wisdom of a different sort, being in your company. Did you see how I lost the soldier they sent to follow after us?" Ari could imagine this fellow's head growing bigger in proportion to the perceived skills he possessed.

"The One True God appears to be on our side, giving aid to our endeavor and helping us to avoid detection," a smooth voice rumbled, thoroughly discrediting the other fellow's imaginary prowess. While the children listened to the *other* version of the event as it transpired, Martha's eyes widened. According to the talebearer, a sudden fog appeared, thick as a cloud, and grew more so as they traveled. It became so impenetrable that they nearly despaired of exiting its density. All at once, the way became clear, and they stepped out of the smoky substance. They saw they had been deposited, fortuitously, near the road that led to their current hiding place. The speaker surmised that the same providence that completely concealed their whereabouts from the soldier who hunted after them, also thwarted further efforts to find them. However else could it be explained? On this, the entire group seemed to agree. Even the braggart grunted in concession. It certainly did sound like an act of divine intervention. Who then, Martha wondered, were these men to justify such an act?

The man with the golden voice continued (there was just no other way to describe it), melodic and mesmerizing. After finding that they had escaped the king's man altogether, the group agreed to set up camp rather than return to the inn where they'd arranged to spend the night. They felt a measure of safety (if only from the soldiers) in knowing that should they be looked for at the inn, they would not be found. Now, all they had to worry about were robbers. So far they had not been accosted.

"Believe what you will," said the boastful fellow, with a sniff, but his tone clearly said otherwise.

Ari looked to his companions and put a finger to his lips. He moved closer to the source of the tantalizing smells, quickly stuck out his hand and uncovered a satchel. He grabbed at the opening greedily, but instead of food, his hand landed in something grainy. Which was promptly scattered as

Ari was grabbed by the scruff of his neck and shaken. Caught again – for the second time in one night.

****

"Let me go! Let me go!" Ari cried. His legs twisted on the ground uselessly as he struggled. He was shaken by the fisted hand in the collar of his tunic once more for his trouble. This man was tall, and Ari's feet barely touched the ground. Still, he fought with everything that was in him. No! Not again – he would not be taken so easily this time. Besides, he was tired of being manhandled.

"I'll let you go when your friends show themselves," came the calm reply. "It's over," he called to Mal and Martha in the darkness. "Come on out, eavesdroppers!" He added as an afterthought, "No injury will come to you or your friend." Meanwhile, all bickering between his cohorts had

79

ceased altogether. His companions had turned their attention to Ari.

Indeed, had the man wanted to harm Ari, he could have done so by now. It was plain that he intended no physical injury to their friend, for he merely held Ari aloft at arm's length so that Ari's punches and kicks would be ineffective. Mal hesitantly stepped forward into the light, his palms out, to show that he meant no harm either. Martha followed closely behind, and Mal made sure to shield her with his body as she hid behind him. For her part, Martha gladly conceded his effort to protect her.

"Let us first see you," Mal countered. A torch was presented by another at the campsite who placed it between Mal and the man who held Ari, lighting the features of both. Mal recognized the man by the kohl markings around his eyes as one of the four from the palace. The Egyptian had removed his wig, though. His head was altogether bald underneath.

"What do you want from us?" Mal demanded even though he was in no position to make demands. But he would come no closer until he knew the fellow's full intentions.

The man sighed. "We would just like to know what you have overheard. It was not for your ears. You may have put yourselves in jeopardy, just by being *nosy*." That last part was said with disgust like he was mad at himself for having been overheard and at them for having the temerity to accomplish it. "It was not for your ears," he repeated. "No good could come of knowing these things," he insisted.

"Well, good way to intimidate them, Horus! Of course, they're not going to tell the truth now!" A diminutive figure ceased stalking back and forth in front of the small fire, likely trying to wear a groove into the ground from worry, to accuse the tall Egyptian.

"H-how else are we to question them, Anil, since you know all about it?" The aggravation in Horus' voice was evident.

"I know that this is not the way! And you shouldn't have just snatched the boy up like that – look at him! He's terrified!" They took the high pitched voice that responded to be Anil. Ari stopped resisting when he saw he had the other man's sympathy.

"And hungry to add – probably just wanted to steal some food. Really Horus, you always overreact," a lazy voice chimed in. Ari couldn't see him clearly, but his was the hand that had given Horus the torch. Ari supposed the voice of this interjector could only be the curly-haired man with the cinnamon-colored hands because he recalled the rings displayed prominently on his fingers.

"Babar, what have you to do with this? At least, I know how and when to act while you just sit there looking helpless!" Horus was really worked up now. Poor Ari was caught in the middle. He looked back and forth, trying to distinguish their features in the light of the fire. Truly, it was becoming increasingly more difficult to keep track of who said what, but Ari had accounted for the name of all but one. "Sulayman – what have you to say?"

"I say, the enemy of my enemy is my friend." The children supposed the musical baritone to be that of the aforementioned Sulayman. *There!* There he is, thought Ari, identifying the last of the noblemen. This had to be the big man, wide almost as he was tall.

"Huh? What's that supposed to mean?" Horus sounded confused. He mumbled something about "being with this group" and how they were "always speaking in riddles."

"I mean," Sulayman clarified, "we have a common enemy. We outmaneuvered the young soldier and, by the looks of it, these young ones have just left the Roman guards' outpost. I've a feeling these children don't want to run into that lot again, either. No telling what the soldiers would do to unescorted children; maybe even press them into service. So I doubt these boys will be carrying tales back to them. In any case, we're safe till morning." He yawned. It was a huge assumption, but he seemed sure of his assessment.

"And," he continued, "there's nothing to be done for it now – whether they know or nil, whether they'll speak on it or not." He walked over to the bag Ari had disturbed and looked down. "The one thing we may presume is that they're hungry. I suggest you give them something to eat and turn in for the night. We'll sort it out tomorrow." And with those words, he turned his back to them as if there were no more to say on the subject and readied for bed.

He took off his robe and busied himself arranging it before stretching out on the ground with his feet to the fire. Maybe that speech had taken a lot out of him. They saw his feet cross, looking for all the world as if he hadn't a care.

The other men soon followed his example, leaving the children standing with a wide-eyed, horror-stricken looking Horus. They could see clearly now by the fire's light, the whites of his kohl-rimmed eyes. How, Horus wondered aloud, did he get stuck with the children? He muttered some words under his breath about not taking a job like this again, shoved flat bread loaves into their hands and turned to make his preparations for sleep, as well.

The children stood dumbfounded by this turn of events. Faced with nothing else to do but follow Sulayman's example, they curled up in a heap for warmth (for the night had grown chilly), nibbling on their bread. They figured this was as good a place to rest as any. A heavy woolen cloth landed on them, flung by Horus. A kindness, they realized. It was an additional covering for warmth. They snuggled under it gladly. Martha, sandwiched between the backs of the two boys, soon fell asleep.

Chapter Nine

Martha awakened to a hard knob pressing into her scalp. Ugh! She was lying on an exposed tree root, the knot of which protruded and dug into her skin. Then, her hair became entangled when she tried to rise. To make matters worse, a rock scraped into her side as she attempted to get free. Martha carefully disentangled her hair, noting the aches and pains she suffered from sleeping on so hard a surface with no barrier to ease her discomfort.

She silently promised herself that when she got back home, she would be more appreciative of the extra goatskins used for her bedding. Truthfully, if this kept happening, she might even take to keeping one on her person for occasions such as this. The Young Master, it appeared, was given to sending them on random jaunts. May as well get used to it and act in advance, as if they could be taken at any time.

Martha was well acquainted with the sounds of breakfast preparations, but when she rested on her elbows and looked around, there was nothing familiar to greet her. The four men went about their morning ablutions, oblivious to Martha. She shut her eyes tight, reclined once more and tried to go back to sleep. She didn't want to rise before Ari and Mal; she didn't feel quite brave enough to face their hosts alone. But the rising sun beat down mercilessly upon her eyelids. That, coupled with the offending tree root, was enough to disturb her return to slumber. Then, there was the smell of food wafting through the air, tempting her taste buds – how could she be expected to sleep through all of that? She gave Ari a nudge with her elbow, then shoved at Mal's back. Neither budged nor stirred, except to mumble incoherently. Sorry protectors they both turned out to be. What if she were in trouble? It was a good thing she didn't need their help, Martha mumbled to herself, and she sat up.

Their benefactors were posed around a small cooking fire, talking. And *eating*. She hardly noticed otherwise, for that very action consumed her. Food, just the thought tantalized, and her stomach grumbled at the memory. She was grateful for the meager provision last night and still held in her hands the remnants of the bread Horus had given them. She had fallen asleep before she could finish, but it was inedible now. She eyed the crumbs lying on her tunic in distaste, knowing with certainty that they were embedded in her cheek, as well. Martha gave up the battle with her appetite and sat up, in hopes that some breakfast yet remained.

"No," Horus was saying. "Our agreement was to be a guide for the three of you – not to babysit children, too." He was tall and lean and muscular, Martha noticed. He'd shed some of his borrowed clothing during the night and wore several pieces of fabric girded about his hips that reached his knees. She was mesmerized by the colorful turquoise neckpiece and golden cuffs at his wrist, the only adornments of his upper body. "How am I to provide protection for you *and* them? It is too much!" As he aired his frustrations, he attached his *klafta,* with its striped fabric falling down his back, to protect his bare head from the rising sun.

"But of course, we'll have to take them with us," the smallest of them insisted hotly. By his high-pitched tone, she knew him to be Anil. So intent were the men in their conversation that they didn't immediately notice Martha. She was able to take in the whole of the argument, unobserved. The fellow continued, "We can't just leave them here for someone to stumble upon them and the information they now have!" He had a hooked nose, which was surprisingly large on one so small and made Martha think more kindly on her own offender. The tunic he wore was simple and neat, but when he belted his waist with a broad strip of finely twined linen, it made him appear even shorter. Also, his back seemed to hunch abnormally. This morning, his head wrap sat high and secure atop his head.

"Anil, why don't we first determine what it is they know before we jump to conclusions?" This came from a man with a profusion of hair that curled wildly about his head. While his hair seemed to be very active, the rest of him remained at rest. This must be Babar, of the sleepy voice.

Martha knew she shouldn't eavesdrop, at least not on this group. They seemed most upset about it last night. But providing a meal was something they should do, she felt, as the men seemed reluctant to leave without them. For the time being, after all, they (she, Ari, and Mal) were in the care of these men. She felt more certain when she thought it over, which made her feel bold and less timid. So she cleared her throat to gain their attention and announced her presence:

"May I have something to eat?"

The men froze at the sound of a maiden's voice, sweetly lilting into the air about them and in direct contrast to the strident tones carried in their masculine offering. At her question, the men whirled in her direction, taking in her brightly colored outer garment and its undoubtedly feminine ornamentation. Unlike Mal and Ari's striped versions, her blue robing was embellished with intricate embroidery.

Mouths fell open. Closed. Opened, again. The silence became so complete that her words seemed to resound for some time after she had stopped speaking. Anil fought for words before he finally sputtered:

"Wh ... why, it's a *girl*!"

****

"I can see she's a girl," Sulayman's deep voice rumbled, from the throat of a chocolate man. His voice, as his clothing, was like silk. His profile revealed skin that was unmarred, without blemish. Martha glimpsed the contrast of white teeth as he spoke though she didn't catch him looking in her direction. She extended her neck and checked the back of his head. No set of eyes peered back at her through the short nest of tight black curls. He, at least, appeared calm and unaffected by the turn of events.

"Of course, she's a girl – what else would she be?" This came from Babar, accompanied by a chuckle.

"Well, this can't be! This won't do at all – this simply will not work!" Anil glared at Babar's attempt to lighten the situation. He shook his head slowly from side to side as though debating internally and still coming up with the same answer. "No. No. No." He punctuated each no with a negative sway of his head, pacing back and forth. "What else could go wrong?"

"No one said anything about including a maiden on our journey," Horus interjected. In the daylight, she could see his kohl markings more clearly. With an incline of his head and a pointed look in Martha's direction, Babar handed a robe to Horus. Horus snatched up the robe and hurriedly threw it over his torso while he fretted. "This certainly makes things more difficult. A lone girl traveling with a group of men is bound to make us more conspicuous than before!"

Martha still sat on the ground, looking stymied at all the tumult she had caused. Ari and Mal slumbered on, oblivious to the disturbance. How could they sleep through this? And she was indignant. She couldn't see how she could make them stand out any more than they already did, for they were a motley assortment to begin with. But she didn't bother to interrupt Horus as the others seemed to take no note of his objections. He ultimately gave up, sat on a rock and decided that he would let them debate until they wore themselves out. The Egyptian rested his elbow on his knee and took up a spectator pose, placing his head in his palm as he watched his travel companions' verbally spar over what to do about Martha.

"Well, of course, it will work," Babar soothed the agitated Anil with his sleepy voice as though compelling Anil to share in his restful state. "It has to work."

Anil would not be comforted. "But all of my careful planning in the night didn't take into consideration that she wasn't one of us!"

Babar countered with, "Who else would she be, besides who she is?"

Anil stopped speaking long enough to give Babar a hard squinty eye. Horus saw his opportunity and jumped in.

"Well, I assumed–"

"And therein lies the problem," Sulayman's voice, smooth and velvety like his skin, commanded all of their attention. "Our assumptions were obviously not based on fact; otherwise, we should have come to a much different conclusion." Horus fumed at being shut down so effectively. He stewed silently as he had no rebuttal and decided to take it out on the sleeping boys.

"You there! Wake up – the both of you!" Horus stalked across the short distance that separated them and nudged the lumps on each side of Martha with a sandaled foot until they stirred. "Get up! So that there'll be no more assumption, let's see who and what you all are in the light of day." Martha sat between Mal and Ari while they were shaken awake.

"They are who they're supposed to be," Babar retorted.

"Don't start with that again," said Horus.

Chapter Ten

Martha, they had already deemed, would raise eyebrows as she was the sole female in their company. It was determined, after much debate, to put Martha in Anil's clothing as he was closest in size to her. Well, not so that he was equal in size, but he was the smallest of them and had extra garments, whereas Mal and Ari did not. His clothes were still too big, even though Martha had kept her tunic on underneath. Following Anil's example, she used a strip of cloth to gird herself in such a way that she appeared to be bulkier in size.

"Well?" She stretched her arms out wide. Anil twirled his finger and directed her to turn around for their inspection. A good sized swath of the drab colored cloth hung from her arm and swallowed up her person. Martha didn't think it would fool anyone, but it was worth a try. She definitely didn't feel any manlier.

"How about this?" She reached behind her and pulled one of the folds of cloth over her head, concealing her face, almost entirely. The men breathed a sigh of relief. When Martha grinned back at them, only her teeth showed.

****

The party set out shortly after breakfast, extinguishing the cooking fire and removing all traces of their camp. Anil determined it best to join up with the large caravan he had seen upon their arrival in *Yerushalaim*. It made sense to affix oneself to a group of travelers whenever possible as it lessened the chance of attack and increased the likelihood of arriving at your destination in peace.

The four pilgrims knew they had been lucky last night, (or blessed, as Sulayman was wont to say) in that they had survived the night unmolested. They attributed that, in part, to the arrival of the children, which increased their numbers. In effect, this provided a deterrent to being plundered by thieves of a lesser number. Indeed, they knew the arrival of the children could have resulted in a much different scenario (foes instead of friends), leading to dire consequences.

The hopes of the men laid also in losing themselves amongst other travelers. The "boys", Mal, Ari and (to those less discerning), Martha, should not raise immediate concerns even if they were stopped. Martha's appearance, at first glance, should not give cause for others to gawk at their assemblage. In any case, the king's soldiers were looking for only four men. Their group had now grown to seven.

The little-used road they'd stumbled upon last night provided a general direction, and they found they were still within the city limits. Unfortunately, they were still uncomfortably near the barracks of the Roman soldiers so they moved quickly to increase the distance between them.

Horus led the way, narrowly missing encounters with uniformed guards. Burrowing further into the city, their eager eyes scanned ahead for signs of the handlers who facilitated passage via caravan.

The children followed the men through the busy streets until they came upon the inn where the men should have spent last night. The men met with the innkeeper and paid him his due for their room and for housing their animals. The camels were then retrieved and loaded with parcels. Some contained food, the children knew, while others held products that were somewhat reminiscent of the fragrances used at the temple during worship. The pack animals seemed not to mind their burden as they trod the ground. Indeed, their load was now lighter because their riders chose to walk alongside Mal, Ari, and Martha.

Looking about them, the children looked for the things and sights they would be familiar with. The marketplace was still there (or should they say, already there), its shops and booths lined up with their goods on display. Though the wares were not as bountiful as during their time, they were pleasing to the eye just the same. Attendants shouted to gain their attention and their patronage. Trinkets, food, fresh fish, smoked meats, delicacies – all were arranged in the marketplace for the review of passersby.

"Pomegranates! Sweet as you have never tasted!" One vendor called to them as they passed, in an attempt to entice the group with his array of produce. Some of the stall attendants, the children couldn't help but notice, were younger versions of sellers they recognized. Others were unknown occupants of booths who, they supposed, were gone by Ari, Mal and Martha's lifetime. In unspoken accord, the troupe made their way with their heads down so as to avoid attracting unnecessary notice. Their destination was a hostel on the other side of the marketplace where the four men hoped to engage with the caravan. The sun was rising higher in the sky, and the men hurried with the children close on their heels, hoping they were not too late.

Martha, swathed in all her fabric, could barely see beyond the cloth covering her head as she scurried after them. She stubbed her toe and collided with a booth, causing it to sway and nearly topple. Before the proprietor set it to rights, she glanced up at his face. Her eyes grew wide with recognition as he glared back at the group of strangers. Martha gulped and put out her hand, apologetically, in an attempt to diffuse the shopkeeper's ire. His was a face she remembered – he was unkind, at best, even during her time.

"Hold! You think can upset my store and just keep walking?" came the question, brusquely. The look he returned held no knowledge of Martha, of course. He was curmudgeonly, even in his youth; that much Martha could see. She ducked her head and refrained from responding, not wanting to give away her disguise. Her hand retreated, turtle-like, into the folds of her outer garment.

"See here!" Horus came to her rescue and distracted the shopkeeper smoothly. "No harm done," he said to the owner as he pressed a coin into his hand.

"What trouble goes here?" A thick soldier approached, charged with keeping the peace, Martha surmised. Her heart fell into her stomach, and she knew she would be the downfall of them all. Anil had been right.

"No trouble, *munifex*," the shopkeeper agreed as he transferred the coin to his other hand. With his right hand, he urged them along. "All is well," he beamed a false, bright smile at the foot soldier, satisfied that he had been adequately compensated for the near mishap.

Gratefully, Martha sped along, head down in her haste to put space between herself and the booth.

The voluminous cloth still encumbered her and wreaked havoc with her field of vision, but she dared not pull it back from her head lest she reveal herself. But she couldn't see. Martha chanced to lift up the overhanging fabric and was glad she did. She came to such an abrupt halt that Ari and Mal collided in an attempt to keep from knocking her over. And then they saw what she saw. Julius, Ari's dad, was before them standing in the midst of the bustling commerce center.

Chapter Eleven

Ari turned his head quickly and busied himself looking at the wares of the nearest stall. *How much for these?* He gestured at the attendant. He didn't trust himself to speak for fear his voice would betray him. Ari fingered the dainty figurines as though they were of great interest to him. Mal joined him, ducking his head and concealing his face. He assumed Martha was behind him. Meanwhile, the attendant gave them a sharp look as they handled items for which they couldn't possibly have a use.

But Martha was not behind Mal, as he supposed. She stood rooted to the spot, gawking at Julius. The resemblance to Ari was even more apparent in the day's light. Ari and Mal wanted to snatch her back when they saw she had not followed them but didn't want to draw more attention to her stupor. As yet, Julius had not noticed her. However, the boys could not hide their distress as they waited to see what would become of them.

"Ah! I have what you need over here," the attendant called and took matters, and Martha, into his own hands, ushering her to the booth where she could join her friends. This caught the attention of Ari's father. He looked up from his conversation and took in the sight of them. Julius narrowed his eyes, looking at them sharply before his attention was diverted by his fellow soldier. The shop's attendant continued to shepherd the group around the back of his booth, putting his back between the children and Julius, obscuring the soldier's vision.

When they'd completely left Julius' field of vision, the shop attendant's friendly mannerism changed. He whispered to them angrily:

"I don't know what you have done, but if you try to hide at my shop again, I will turn you in *myself!*" He gave the group of them a shove. "Go away – and do *not* come back!" He harrumphed, turned from them and went back to selling his wares.

111

Ari, Mal, and Martha almost didn't know what to make of that. The man, even though he'd treated them roughly at the end, apparently thought he was saving them from being caught by the Roman government and being punished for some crime. Even though they'd committed none, they appreciated his quick action. The Roman government, after all, was not given to forgive offenses, even if they were only perceived.

The children were more inclined to think kindly of him despite the rude way he'd shoved them. In reality, he'd pushed them out of harm's way. They watched his retreating back, noticing just then that he had a slight limp. He had the look of a particular man, a peddler from their time.

"Isn't that–" recognition dawned on Mal's features. Before he could finish, another voice interrupted.

"There they are ..." The children jumped with a start and were about to flee when they saw Horus. His powerful strides energetically ate up the distance between himself and the children, his charges right on his heels. The scholars were evidently accustomed to a more sedentary life. To varying degrees, the faces of Anil, Sulayman and Babar showed the effort exerted in keeping pace with Horus. But, keep up, they did; Anil's steps marched double-time to avoid being left behind. Martha's audible sigh was filled with relief at the sight of them. She had wondered if they'd been deserted by their former hosts.

She figured they would have been afraid that their capture would lead to the demise of the entire venture. Their expressions reflected her own; glad that the children escaped detection, happy that they'd avoided being detained.

Chapter Twelve

Since they'd been spotted by Ari's father – unknown as such to the four men, but viewed as a threat just the same – the consensus was to avoid the caravan altogether and continue their journey alone. The group left through the nearest gate, without further delay, camels and children in tow.

Despite their rush to leave *Yerushalaim*, the party stopped shortly thereafter. They even lingered near the entrance for quite some time, hidden from plain sight, while taking a cold meal of dates, figs, and soft goat cheese. They were quiet as they ate, each lost in their thoughts. Mal was frustrated because he felt they should be doing *something*. Martha was accepting of their situation because nothing could be done until they were led *what* to do. And Ari's mind was elsewhere, on his father. He busied himself by using his gift, unobtrusively, to call water to him from out of the ground, under the rocks and wherever he sensed it. Soon he had a small puddle at his feet. He drew his sandaled foot through it, distractedly.

Horus left his charges for a short while and went back to the marketplace alone to secure additional provisions for their journey. (He deemed himself the craftiest of the group and least likely to get caught.) The days were short during this season and by the time Horus had returned, the day was far spent. It was nearing evening when they set out again. It appeared to the children as if Horus and the men drew the time out on purpose, waiting for something.

****

Once they'd committed themselves to including the children, the four men had become quite amicable. They freely answered questions and opened up about their lives while walking down the cobbled road.

"We are all considered men of wisdom in our homelands," Sulayman offered candidly, in his deep melodic voice. "I am the ruler of my people, and many learned men have traveled to my kingdom for insight into their problems." He nodded in Anil's direction.

"Anil, you have already met." The little man inclined his head in acknowledgment of the introduction. The *klafta* was draped loosely across his head and held in place with a cord. Without the added height of his formal headdress, he was surprisingly small. Sulayman continued, "He is a scholar, a man of many letters and languages, a student of the stars. In fact, it was upon consulting him that we came on this journey. Horus, you also know. He is our guide as we move through foreign territory. He will lead us to the city we seek." This was met with a grunt from Horus. "And Babar – don't let his jesting nature fool you." Babar gave them a wink and a beaming smile, looking harmless.

"He is a favored prince among his people and easily the cleverest among us."

"But I have wisdom of a different sort," Horus interjected, offense in every timbre of his voice that he had not been included in their ranks of intelligence. "Something that money and learning at *ti anzeeb* cannot provide. You can't even be born into it," he added smugly. "This kind can only be earned!" He sneered at the others, rendering their brand worthless in his eyesight. "I have been on my own since I was a child. I am very wise to this world and knowledgeable about the ways of people."

"Ah! But even the journey of life can provide admirable instruction," Babar rejoined. "Sometimes, it is the very best school we can ever attend. Experience can be a worthy instructor, and you may, very well, be the sharpest of us all."

Sulayman didn't respond but looked at the children from under raised eyebrows as if to say, *"See?"*

The children could see the good judgment Babar exercised in agreeing with Horus and elevating him to the same level as the others. It was just plain smart. *More flies can be gained with honey than vinegar*, as the adults were given to say. Horus was receptive to Babar's veiled act of diplomacy and inclined his head in Babar's direction, who nodded back. It was immediately evident that Horus was mollified and thus, bound to feel validated, be more cooperative and less competitive or resentful of their accomplishments because of Babar's quick intervention. Horus sniffed his offense at the rest of the group but was already placated and less disagreeable.

"But where are we going?" Ari asked of their guide. "What city do you seek?" Perhaps he and his friends could be of assistance, as well.

"We are headed for—" Horus drew up sharply and checked himself at the clearing of Anil's throat, "a neighboring town," he finished. "A small city, indeed – which should be of no concern to yourselves, really." He gave a small smile and tried to say it in such a way as to remain friendly. Obviously, their hosts thought the less the children knew, the better. But Horus looked like he was about to explode with the effort of keeping it to himself. "What use is it *not* to tell them?" he broke out, turning on the men. "They all KNOW where we are going! The king knows; his men know – they told US where to go!" He turned back to the children, shaking his head and grumbling something about "secrets."

"It's better they not know, Horus," Anil insisted. He spoke softly, instead of hysterically as he had been on the subject up until then. "No good can come of it. If we are captured or are separated, what they know may bring us all to ruin. We have seen the king's face and his demeanor in this matter. You said it yourself; the king cannot be trusted." Anil, too, shook his head somberly. "Let us leave it for now. All will be made known soon. Then we can be done with our fellowship and perhaps avoid bringing destruction upon all of our heads."

To this speech, the group nodded. It did seem the wisest choice. Even the children, though puzzled, agreed. Soon they would know anyway. What did it matter that the men did not want to discuss it? The children were familiar with the layout of the land, in any case. They knew well the direction in which they were headed and the city to which this road led. The path, populated with trees, was often used by those who went on pilgrimages to *the* Temple during feasts and holy days. Martha recalled the road from her travels with family to visit her aunt. She knew what she would find when they arrived; David's Well and Rachel's Tomb, for these landmarks were ancient. The question was, to what purpose? Martha decided to try an innocuous route.

"Why do you travel?" She gave Anil the big-eyed look that worked so often on her father. When Anil's mouth tamped down as if he were wondering how much to reveal, she tried again. "I mean, how did you come to make this journey? Sulayman said you were visiting him." He really hadn't said but she'd gathered as much. She supposed Anil could answer that without divulging too much.

"Anil came to consult with me after he saw an unusual event in the sky," Sulayman answered her query. "As a man who is constantly sought after for wisdom, I keep myself apprised of the things that make one wise." His smile beamed at them, open and friendly from a face the color of dark spices, his voice rich and velvety smooth. "Anil is knowledgeable regarding the stars but could not fully comprehend the meaning. He decided to pay me a visit. I had also seen the strange occurrence in the heavens, shining like a star – but it was not! It *moved* in a peculiar manner. I was puzzled, too until Anil hit upon something that caused me to delve into the holy scriptures." Sulayman was caught up in a fever now, the spirit of adventure blazing in his eyes. Anil smiled at that and nodded in remembrance.

"I said it seemed to herald the birth of a great king," Anil recalled, excitedly.

"I was drawn into the tale also by Anil," Babar remarked in his sleepy voice. "I have been his willing student, ever since I was about your ages. Under his tutelage, I have learned much about the heavens and nature, but also of court life, palace intrigue and political alliances."

"And he has always been an apt pupil," Anil broke in. He gave Babar a fatherly pat on his shoulder, reaching up to do so. Pride was evident in his voice. Babar smiled in response and continued.

"Ordinarily, I'm not a valiant sort, but I was determined to contribute to this noble undertaking and see the result. I couldn't resist. I'm curious." He tilted his head, lifted his hands and shrugged as if to say that explained his part in it all.

"Wait – you mean you're *following* the star?" Mal was incredulous. He wasn't a learned man such as these, but this much he knew from time spent in the boat with his father. Fishermen navigated by the sky and used the heavens to interpret the weather. Of course, a star could be used for direction, but these men implied that a star was *leading* them. That didn't sound quite right. He said as much to the men.

"Ah! But this one *does*," Anil rebutted and took up the story, unable to contain himself any longer. His face turned rapturous. "It moves, it leads, it guides, unlike anything we have ever seen!" His hands punctuated each phrase with a flourish, waving wildly in the air. "It led us here," he sobered suddenly. "I believe – WE believe – something special happened on the day we all saw that star. An event such as this means that the heavens, and our world, is forever changed."

"We have come to see for ourselves," Babar added somberly, "that we may be witnesses and testify to its truth." He was serious, for a change.

"We have come to worship and pay homage due to a king," Sulayman said. "As it is foretold in the prophecy: Behold, a virgin shall conceive!"

Martha knew that saying. Every young maiden was made aware that she could be *the one*. The claim made Martha a little apprehensive, yet anticipatory. She loved her baby sister and thought her adorable. One day, Martha supposed she would be mother to her own. But she wasn't ready to be *the one* just yet.

"But how is this possible?" Babar queried, shaking his head at the impossibility. "If this were true …" his voice trailed off as he speculated on the implications. It appealed to the purist in him. Unlike Anil, who was a purveyor of the movement of the stars, Babar was a devotee of the movement of all things in nature and how they worked. An occurrence like this did not just happen, *ever*. The thought of it was one of the few things that could rouse him from his usual state of calm. "That such a," he stammered here, his mind reeled as he struggled for words, "a *marvel* would take place …" He was quite at a loss to express himself on the matter. It went against all reason, everything he held to be true.

"I do not know how," Sulayman admitted, expelling a heavy sigh. "The holy writings of Esaias declare:

For unto us a child is born, unto us a son is given: and the government shall be upon his shoulder: and his name shall be called Wonderful, Counselor, The mighty God, The everlasting Father, The Prince of Peace.

It is an event for which my people have long awaited," Sulayman finished.

"Wait," Mal jumped in, a little startled at this bit of information. Like Martha, he recalled this well-known scripture. It had to do with the coming of the Anointed One. "How is it that you know the holy writings of *my* people?" Obviously, this Sulayman was a scholar and studied many things. But these were the sacred writings of Mal's forefathers. Why did Sulayman say they were of *his* people?

"That is another matter to discuss," Sulayman smiled widely at Mal and the other children. "Too much for me to go into a history lesson." He touched Mal's shoulder in brotherly fashion. "Suffice to say, we are distant cousins – my people and yours. We are keepers of the same covenant, children of the One True God, and protectors of his holy relics." Sulayman stopped short as if he were about to say more. He bit back the words and mentally berated himself for his loose tongue.

"The heavens have also declared his birth," Anil covered for Sulayman, suspected that the ruler had already given away more than he ought. But such is the manner of secrets. They have a way of coming out at the most inopportune moments. Anil continued, "It created such a spectacle that it announced his arrival. Born the king of this land, the stars reveal he is Lord of all!" Anil's eyes gleamed fervently. "Now we have come to see, we must witness this great miracle for ourselves!"

The children and Horus looked upon the men, who had come to a full stop, eyes lifted to the heavens as if looking for a star that leads. Martha was puzzled. How could such an event happen, only decades before they were born, and they not be made aware? Their present day king, Herod Antipas, was not an authentic heir to the throne according to the adults. He wasn't of the right bloodline, being neither royal nor even of *Yisra'el.* King Herod was successor to his father. Both were figureheads for the Roman government, which was why their legions occupied the land. These two kings were known to be bloody rulers. Martha had heard of their deeds; their ilk was unworthy of the devotion of these men. Surely, neither of these kings were able to inspire, but only command fealty. Could it be that this child was descended from King David and destined to rule Judea? And how had Martha, Ari, and Mal not known, nor heard of him? Whatever happened to him?

A sniffling sound broke through her reverie, and she looked to see Anil's downturned head. His visage was cloaked in sadness and a tear rolled down his cheek. Puzzled even more thoroughly at his silent weeping, she touched his face gently.

"Why do you cry?" His sorrow touched her and made her feel sad, too.

"We have lost sight of the star," he wept more openly now. "We came to the capital of this nation, seeking an audience with the king. With no star to guide us, we faltered. We came, expecting to take our part in a celebration of the arrival of a new heir. Reason dictated that it had to be the birth of his son, but it was not so! The king has had no new son." Anil straightened his posture and looked up mournfully at the sky as he spoke. "I fear that our visit has only brought trouble upon this land, as we have alerted the king to the birth of a rival for his throne. The true king."

"We must reach him first. And warn him," Sulayman said gravely.

"And move surreptitiously, so as not to lead the king and his men directly to him," Babar added.

"And, I must find another way out to lead these men back home," Horus admitted his part. "For they cannot go back the way they came. It would mean certain death to the child and maybe for these men, as well." The weight of it all showed on the faces of the foreigners. A cause that began with such promise had now become grim because of the consequences should they fail.

"I should have paid more attention to that dream!" Anil suddenly blurted, shaking his fist. "I should have known never to go to the palace."

"You could not have known, teacher," Babar spoke comfortingly. "How were you to decipher the images correctly?"

"THIS IS MY LIVELIHOOD," Anil railed. "It is my duty and my pleasure to instruct kings on dreams and such matters. As a trusted advisor, I have been privy to certain information that could ruin nations, but my discretion failed me in this most important matter of all!"

"You are too hard on yourself, Anil," Sulayman's deep voice countered. "I, myself, believed your interpretation of the dream to be true." Sulayman turned to the children and elaborated for their benefit, for they may as well know all.

"Anil dreamed of wild beasts and a great dragon, at a king's residence, waiting to pounce on a child. He assumed, as did we all, that we were to go to the palace to warn the king that such a danger was imminent for his child."

"Sadly," Anil spoke from his downcast expression, "this was not the case, at all. I fear that the king IS the dragon and his men ARE the wild beasts, waiting to devour the child."

Martha, Mal, and Ari stood with their mouths agape in shock, and the full burden of the secret settled on them, too.

"Now you know why we journey," Anil concluded.

"Come, let us be on with it," said Horus. He gathered the reins of Anil's camel, forgotten in his distress. "We will reach *Beth Lechem* by nightfall."

Chapter Thirteen

Ari trudged along the dusty, rock-strewn road with Mal and Martha on either side of him. He didn't speak much to his friends, for too much was on his mind. Nothing that would be new to them, he imagined. The questions hadn't changed: Why were they here? But he wasn't overly concerned with the answer to that, strangely enough – he felt like it would be revealed in time. He had weightier matters to deal with that overshadowed their purpose for being here.

Although he'd longed for his father and to see him once more, to be here and not be able to converse with him was a lot to absorb. His father was within walking distance, but rather than go to him, Ari had run away instead. A world where Julius did not know him as his son was unimaginable. A tear welled up in his eye, and Ari fought back the urge to cry. Water threatened to spill over anyway, but Ari found, by some quirk of his gift, that he could quell the tears that threatened to spill and redirect the water so that his eyes remained dry. Hmmm. His attention was diverted elsewhere when Ari saw a lump appear on his arm, tickling downward to his hand.

"Huh?" He must have spoken aloud for Mal and Martha looked at him, curiously. He clamped his mouth and shook his head. Martha's eyes widened as she understood what he could not say among their hosts, *not now – later*.

Ari willed the fluid back up his arm to be reabsorbed somewhere, he assumed, in his upper body. He visualized that salty liquid remaining isolated and revolving slowing inside the dome that was his head. But, that wasn't happening, truly? He knew he could control water outside of his body, but also within? Ari visualized the ball of fluid, imagining that it remained contained as it moved. He caused it to resurface and travel, again, down his arm, all the way to his fingertips. His index finger appeared swollen as if he had struck it (he had done that a few times while hammering tent pegs with his uncles). Ari willed the excess liquid away by forming a mental picture of the water draining away from his hand.

Martha smothered a giggle, entertained at his feat. Mal heard Martha's muffled sound and turned. A look of horror crossed his face as he saw what Ari was doing. A lump swept across Ari's forehead, like a pendulum, swinging back and forth. It swung right, then left, following the pattern of his eyes.

Stop, Mal's stern message was written on his face. Ari responded with a grin and directed the ball to halt in the middle of his head. At Ari's cross-eyed expression, Mal wanted to laugh but merely shook his head instead. Ari could be so silly sometimes. Just then, Ari stubbed his foot on a stone on the path, causing him to stumble. He flailed a little, trying to regain his composure, which was almost Martha's undoing.

Previously ignored by their hosts, this drew a look back by their guide. Horus gave them a piercing look, craning his neck to view them, but all he received was their angelic expressions in reply. But what more did he expect from children? Assured that all was well, he turned around, continuing to lead his charges on their journey.

Martha hung her head, the swath of cloth engulfing her head altogether as she shook with silent laughter. Mal purposefully stared straight ahead and refused to laugh because he knew his big, hearty boom would draw further attention. Ari snickered next to him then grew quiet. Curious, Mal turned to him. Now it was Ari's turn to look appalled. Mal and Martha followed the direction of his finger as he pointed to the ground. Their expressions grew sober, too, when they saw that Ari's previously engorged finger appeared to be withered, as skin sometimes did when you were immersed in water too long, only more severely. Ari lifted his hand up, curiously, to observe what was, to him, even more of a spectacle. He had pulled too much fluid away from his hand.

Ari gulped in dismay and wondered if he could fix what he had done. He concentrated and willed fluid, of any sort to his thirsty limb, for he didn't even know now what had happened to the liquid he'd been playing with. He'd lost his concentration when he stumbled. Ari prayed he hadn't done any permanent damage while toying with his gift. In his mind, he saw the waters in his body rushing to his hand. A relieved look spread across his features when he saw that his body willingly obliged, obediently restoring his finger to its former state. Ari sighed and ducked his head. When he met their eyes, his expression was sheepish. Martha looked concerned, all joviality gone. Mal just shook his head again and turned his gaze towards the path they trod.

****

They truly could have reached the little village much sooner, but their guide took a meandering rocky path, delaying their arrival. When the sun set and darkness covered the sky, his reasoning was made plain. The four men stood with their faces toward heaven, searching the stars anxiously.

"Where are you?" Anil squinted at the twinkling lights, muttering to himself. "We need you to find him!" He gave up grumbling and shouted into the night, demanding, "Show yourself! We need you to help him!" He was sobbing at the star-studded sky now, looking for the one that was unlike all others. The rest of his party searched the sky alongside him, hopefully, for signs of a guiding light. They heard a sharp intake of breath.

"There!" Anil pointed, suddenly ecstatic. "There! There it is!" He jumped up and down for joy. "The light! The light! The star that leads!" Loud sighs of relief were heard all around. It was a welcome sight to the four men and one to which they had become accustomed; but for the children, it was a most unusual occurrence. Their eyes widened as they looked in the direction of Anil's finger and saw the burst of blue light that flared and then burned white. It was more like a flame, in actuality. How, the children thought, could this be?

And then, the "star" was on the move. Their eyes followed the flame as it ambled towards the little town and hovered high in the night sky. Everyone whooped in relief and pressed onward, anxious not to lose sight of the illumination.

Chapter Fourteen

The village square was quiet. In appearance, all had turned in for the night. But the sojourners could see figures moving about by the firelight of the rambling homes with their mud thatched roofs and whitewashed walls. A hostel establishment was readily identifiable by its behemoth proportions, in comparison to the much smaller dwellings. They supposed they could spend the night there, if need be. The glowing flame hovered over the entrance to the little town and was even brighter as they approached. As they passed the homes, the troupe wondered how the city could be unaware that such a sight existed right in their midst. Surely, they could see? Shouldn't this blazing beacon in the sky have drawn the attention of the residents of *Beth Lechem* as it had the travelers? But the villagers carried on with their lives, consumed with their tasks and ignorant to a miracle occurring right outside their very doorsteps. The weary pilgrims saw from the road, a mother holding up her baby in the lamplight. She then cuddled him to her breast.

The flame flickered as if to gain their attention, and then their celestial guide was on the move again. It glided slowly in the sky, ever before them, leading them and providing light for their steps. Then, their view was obscured by a copse of trees. Where did it go? Greedily, each eye of their party searched the darkness to no avail. Their hearts sank, but they stayed on course, following the general direction they were going when they last saw the star. As the village turned sparse, they began to give up hope until, on the outskirts of town, the light appeared again. The flame alighted on a small dwelling, winked again and, seemingly, dropped down inside. That was their best guess for what happened to the flame, for it was no longer visible. If anything, it filled that habitation now and emitted an ethereal glow.

Seven sets of eyes were filled with awe, and the light from within fell on their faces, revealing their wondrous expressions. It was a humble home, from the looks of it, not unlike their own homes, the children thought. Surely, this was not it – not the abode of a king?

"I don't understand-" Martha began but stopped as quickly as she'd begun. This was no kingly habitat, but their hosts were resolved to go wherever this "star" led them. They tied their camels to a nearby post and approached the residence.

Mal, Ari, and Martha hung back, a little uncertain of what they should do now that the moment had arrived. What should one say to a king? Do? How would they greet his family? But time was past for planning their actions in advance. Gathering their nerve, they looked to each other for encouragement.

Mal gave a kind of half grimace, half smile. He looked as they all felt, uncomfortable and unprepared for the moment now that it was upon them. Martha widened her eyes, stretched her neck out and nodded as if to say: *We're here now, and there's nothing to be done about it so let's make the best of it.*

Really, Ari thought. She said all that with her expression, and he had responded with his own – a raised eyebrow, accompanied by a smirk that said, again: Really? His mind took a break from the somberness of the situation to critique her expression and her summation, which was far too mature. Truly, Martha hung around adults too much. Ari's mental wandering was interrupted when he heard movement inside the home, accompanied by the rustle of fabric. Then came a child's giggle and the voice of a woman calling:

"Come away from there, little one," her voice carried beyond the walls to their hearing. "Let *Abba* get the door."

So the occupants knew they were outside and were coming to greet them. They waited at the door quietly, not knocking since their presence was already known. The door opened and a soft light spilled out of the home, filling the entranceway.

Chapter Fifteen

A man stood before them, blocking their vision of mother and child. He wasn't overly large or impressive in appearance. A damp lock of curly hair hung on his forehead as if he had just wiped his face after washing or maybe mopped a damp brow. He looked inquiringly at the group, taking them in with an all-encompassing look. As he looked for a leader or spokesperson among them, his glance fell to Anil, who stood before the group and strained his neck to get a look beyond this fellow barring the door.

"Are you travelers looking for lodging?" the man asked of them; he appeared puzzled by Anil's strange behavior. The man looked down with a wry smile and shook his head at his own question. "Of course, you are travelers," he said with a rueful grin, "for I don't recognize any of you."

The group didn't respond, a little dumbfounded that they were here, at their longed for destination. The children didn't know what to say, and the men seemed in awe. The man gave a little clearing of the throat, uncomfortably, and tried again.

"Do you need lodging?" He spoke slowly. Surely, they couldn't all be simple. "Was there no room at the inn?"

"Ah … uh," Horus was the first of them to attempt speech. "Well, yes – of a sort – uhm," he straightened and debated how much he should reveal of their intentions. "We … are travelers, yes," that much was true. He could attest to that, he thought, with a short nod in the man's direction.

"We are here," Anil had recovered his ability to speak, as his attempts to see beyond the man had been thwarted. He looked up at the man earnestly as he spoke, "We have come to see the child."

Well, Ari thought, so much for subterfuge. He looked at Mal and Martha on either side of him and shrugged. He guessed they were going with the direct approach. Apparently, the man was not at all surprised by Anil's demand for he stepped aside, wordlessly, inviting the party inside.

Not thinking it would be nearly so easy to gain access, the assembly followed the direction of his hand until their eyes rested on a young woman. In age, she wasn't much older than Mal, although she was already a wife and mother. The thought made Martha shudder internally a little. That time was coming for her soon. In only a few years, she would be considered of age – old enough to marry. She wrested her mind away from that thought and took notice of the toddler at the side of the young woman. Clearly, he was the young boy they'd heard while still on the other side of the door. But no babe was present, which made her wonder just how long her new acquaintances had been traveling. She looked more curiously upon the young boy. He returned her look with interest.

"Miriam?" Her husband called to her as he turned in her direction. "We have ... ah ..." He seemed at a loss for what to call them, "Guests." *Be careful to entertain strangers, for you may actually entertain angels unaware.* Hmmm. The husband was well aware of the saying, and this group looked harmless enough, in his estimation. Moreover, it certainly was not the first time, nor, he suspected, the last time that *strangers* would visit his fledgling family.

As protector and provider of their home, even though he judged the assemblage of men (was that a girl among them?) to be innocent, he stood between the group and his family, barring complete access. The husband looked at them with an inquisitive expression that invited the callers to take up their story and explain why they were in his home. For their part, the sojourners wondered that the man of the house didn't seem overly perturbed or even concerned at their visit. He waited patiently for Anil to speak as Anil seemed to be the spokesman for the group. Anil gathered a roll of cloth that he'd retrieved from the camel just before they'd approached the home. He fiddled with it nervously, apologetically.

"We are travelers," he began, "foreigners to this country." He turned and nodded at the others as he continued. "We are great men of renown, too, where we come from. All are leaders amongst our clans and students of wisdom, seekers of knowledge and truth." He cleared his throat at this and stood up a little straighter as he addressed the husband. His introduction seemed to fortify Anil and reminded him of who they all were, their purpose and their own station in life.

"Some time ago, we saw a sign in heaven. A star appeared, lighting up the sky as a flame." His hand traversed the air in front of him as he became caught up in his tale. "A star that *moved*! I, myself, am a stargazer, and I was doing so on that night. Oh!

149

It was a brilliant sight! The like I have never seen!" The hands of the little man were doing aerial acrobatics as he re-enacted his story. I called to my friend," he gestured at Babar, "as he was a guest in my home at the time and showed him this great light." His voice grew hushed, "What could it mean – this sign in the heaven?" With a tilt of his head towards his friend, Anil now included Sulayman in his tale. "We consulted with this ruler, who is venerable and wise, and came to this conclusion: Surely this star heralded a grand event – the birth of someone of significance of such a magnitude that it was written in the heavens themselves." He looked then at the little boy, and his voice became filled with awe. "It was the birth, we came to believe, of a great king."

Without waiting for a response, Anil unfurled the cloth with a flourish and laid it on the floor before the lad, kneeling reverently as he did so.

Craning her neck for a glance over his shoulder, Martha thought, *myrrh*? She recognized the balm from use by her mother. It had a few applications, most notably being used in the preparation of deceased loved ones because it was so fragrant. It was also utilized for its medicinal properties. But why give that to a child? Puzzled at that choice, she turned to view the parcels of her other traveling companions with curiosity. Sulayman and Babar took their cue from Anil and followed suit with similar packages they bore.

"We have traveled a long time to find you, little one," Babar said gently as he knelt with his offering. He unwrapped his package to show gold, lustrous and gleaming, revealed in the folds therein. "May this small token bring comfort and aid to you during your life's travels." His speech was somber, as the occasion, and was infused with ceremony.

"Gifts," Sulayman added as he, too, managed to lower his sizable girth, "fit for One who is our king and priest forever!" Ari recognized this present from the other night when he'd put his hand in the satchel looking for food. No wonder it smelled familiar. It was used during services at the Temple. Sulayman beamed his great smile and lowered his head before the child. There was a sniff, as Sulayman wiped the corner of his eye. Then, with a great cry, he fell to his knees and bowed himself completely to the ground, immense shoulders quaking as he was overcome by the meeting.

"During MY lifetime," Sulayman was heard to murmur over and over, "who would have believed?"

At this point, Ari (and surely, the others) began to feel a little awkward as they had nothing to give. The gifts were soon arranged attractively before the little child. For his part, the little boy tugged on his mother's skirt and looked askance. She looked down at him and made a face, forming an "O" with her mouth. Such a solemn one, Martha thought to herself. Had they not already heard him laugh, she would have thought him incapable. That is until he responded to his mother's expression – he grinned a broad, face-splitting grin. She raised her eyebrows at him, smiled and nodded.

At that, the child detached himself from her side and approached the offerings. He passed his hands over each item, touching, fingering and lifting them to his face to breathe in their fragrance. Frankincense, Ari now realized, was in the satchel he'd disturbed, in his search for food. That seemed such a long time ago, rather than only last night. He didn't know how he'd not recognized it immediately. The features of the little one went rapturous at the smell. Perhaps he recalled it, too.

His face, however, went still at the scent of myrrh. He looked up at his mother, puzzled, his face grown serious again. Such a strange gift to give to a young boy, Ari thought. He would have much preferred a toy, were he in the toddler's shoes, like his wooden pipe. He fingered the little flute he carried on him always, which hung from a string around his neck. On an impulse, he took it off and offered it to the little one, down on one knee. Maybe it wasn't a gift for a king, but certainly fit for a small boy. Caught up in the reverence of the occasion, Horus, Martha, and Mal were on their knees, too, although they had no gift to bring. Merely being in the presence of the little king seemingly commanded their obeisance.

"AGH!" Mal grabbed his head as a fit suddenly overtook him, falling to his side on the floor. His own scream joined those that echoed in his head. His limbs flailed about, flapping the dirt floor like a fish out of water. He wished he could stop, but he couldn't contain himself. He was in agony. Mal looked to the others as he rolled, nearly tossing himself into the fire. Couldn't they hear it, too? But everyone else seemed unaffected. They all wore expressions of helplessness and concern. "Help ..."

was the last word he uttered as he reached toward Ari, Martha, someone, anyone to relieve his distress. Then darkness overtook him.

Chapter Sixteen

Mal came to awareness with a jolt. He was sweating profusely as if in a fever. A soft hand touched his brow. He opened his eyes to Martha's worried expression. She pursed her lips.

"How are you feeling?" Martha asked, worry etching her voice. Ari hovered in the background, looking over her shoulder anxiously.

"Where are we?" Mal croaked, answering her question with his own. He felt better, but only marginally so. His vision was cleared – that is, he didn't see that flame anymore. The voices were a dull drone now, but he felt like the volume could increase at any moment. The disturbing visions had made an indelible impression, however, and panic consumed him. He didn't know what was wrong with him. It was entirely possible that he only had moments, perhaps, before a seizure could take over again.

"We're still in the home of Yosef and Miriam, come to see the child king," she responded. Mal recalled the events leading up until just before he'd passed out. He nodded his head in the darkened room; the absence of light soothed his aching head and calmed his eyes.

He remembered hanging back from the rest of the group after they'd entered the house. He'd tried to appear interested, bobbing his head, he hoped, in all the right places. Mal looked encouragingly at the child as the little one cautiously approached the items laid before him. But his head – again. The buzzing was back, louder than before. It grew ever noisier and drowned out the conversation before him. His head felt as if it were about to split.

And something was wrong with his vision. He must have stared at that flaming star too long, he guessed. It migrated ever before him, still leading him. He didn't think the others saw it because they seemed not to react to its movement. Sometimes the light was on top of the young lad's head. At others, it was directly in the little boy's face. So much so, that the child's features were obscured altogether. All Mal could see then was a flame instead of a face. That image, along with the undercurrent of voices, had combined to give him the worst headache imaginable.

"Mal," Martha had whispered forcefully at him, from her position beside him on her knees, as was he. She noticed Mal wasn't paying attention to any of this. The look on his face said he was elsewhere. He was missing it all, and who knew what any of this was supposed to mean? "Mal, what are you doing?" This, she said to him when she saw how he cast his eyes wildly about the room, his head jerking as if in response to something he heard. No! Not again.

In response, Mal had suddenly grabbed his head and bent over in pain. He was caught up in the voices again. Screams of agony had overwhelmed him.

And then he was here, in this darkened room. Mal didn't yet trust himself to speak but instead, marshaled his strength in anticipation for the battle his words would bring.

"He touched you, and you stilled," Martha was saying now in amazement. Mal searched her face in the dim light, his features a mask of confusion. "The little boy," she elaborated, "he touched you, and you stopped jerking and shouting. You became calm." Mal looked to Ari for confirmation. Ari returned Mal's look with a shrug of his shoulders as if to say: *yes, that happened – no, we don't know why.*

"It was like he had influence over you," Martha was still speaking, Mal realized. She was searching for words; he could tell. "As if he had power over your condition … or whatever it is that's affecting you." She didn't have words to quite describe it completely, all she knew was that Mal had responded to the young boy's touch.

"We ... we have to leave," Mal interrupted her impatiently as the swell of voices began to rise again. Time was running out. He had to tell them – let them know! He looked at Martha like one gone mad and seized her arm, clutching until she made a sound of protest. "We must leave – THEY must go!" His eyes were wild now. "They are coming!" Mal clutched at Martha's arm, squeezing convulsively. "I've seen them," he was sobbing. "I know what they will do to him." His eyes pled with Martha to understand what he tried to convey as Ari pried his fingers loose.

"Sh, sh, sh," Martha touched his face, consoling him as she would her little sister, even though he was her elder cousin. Clearly, he was in no position to take care of her at the moment, so it was left to her to look out for him. But Mal would not be easily quieted.

"You don't understand–" he looked to Ari for help. Mal searched the face of his friend, his eyes darting around in a frenzy. "We must go–" He clutched his stomach suddenly and doubled over, pain evident in his features. Ari grabbed Mal and eased him on his back while Martha peered worriedly over Ari's shoulder. She maneuvered around Ari, clucking her concern over Mal. She caressed his hair as she crooned to him, attempting to provide comfort. Mal breathed through the pain in big, heavy breaths, his eyes staring at the ceiling. For the moment, his mind was on nothing but the pain.

"How is he?" a voice inquired from the doorway. Horus carried a steaming beverage filled with delicate herbs. Martha and Ari looked up at the sound though Mal remained as he was; his gaze unfocused as he panted at the ceiling before him.

Horus looked over the group and took in the situation. Mal sprawled on the dirt floor, sweat beading his forehead – Ari and Martha's with their tight, drawn faces. Horus held out the earthen cup to Martha and asked, "He's doing it again?"

Martha nodded helplessly in response to the query, though it was rhetorical. Mal was in obvious distress, still. She didn't even see the proffered drink as she rocked back and forth, cradling Mal's head in her lap and seeking to console him. He relaxed and went limp in her lap. Her soothing sounds began to have some effect on him.

"He keeps saying we have to leave," Ari said to Horus in a hushed voice, not wanting to get Mal worked up again.

"He may very well be correct in that," Horus replied. "After Anil gave the parents his account of our encounter with the king, the husband became very agitated. He said he had a dream that he took his family and left this place. But he thought it was for another time. Now he feels that the king will come after his son now. Tonight!" he added for emphasis.

"This is bad business, bad indeed – I knew that fellow for a crook from the time I laid eyes on him!" His mouth was a pinched line as he relived their visit to the palatial residence. "I should have–" Horus began, and then shook his head. "What could I do?" He shrugged at Martha and Ari in resignation. "I am merely their guide. I took them where they wanted to go."

Ari let Horus vent for a time, but he still wondered what they could do about Mal. He interrupted Horus, after what seemed a drawn out length of time, and finally asked just that. But Horus had gone quiet and looked beyond him. Ari turned to follow Horus' gaze. Mal was up, standing on his feet and gathering himself together. There was but a touch of the madness on his features though his face was set and determined.

"We are leaving," Mal said, in a voice that brooked no argument. "All of us. NOW! It's not safe for us – for him – here." He looked to Ari and Martha. He seemed almost himself, sober even. They saw their friend at that moment, not the madman he had been acting. His eyes were full of meaning only they would understand. "*We* must protect him."

"Er, well, that is what I came to tell you," Horus said. He was a little puzzled about Mal's comments but didn't dwell on it overmuch given Mal's behavior since their arrival. "We are leaving now. The question is, what can be done with *you*?" He looked at the children before him, feeling somewhat responsible for them. After all, it was at the insistence of the adults that the trio were brought along. They had planned to send the young people on their way once their mission was complete, perhaps even see them to their homes but that seemed doubtful now. They had to leave in haste, making the best of it as they went.

"You go on," Mal asserted, speaking for them all. "We will go with the family." He held his chin up as he spoke, defying any of them to make mention of his seizures. He could do this. He had to. But Horus still looked at him, skeptically. He opened his mouth to object.

Fire whizzed by the elbow of the tall Egyptian so quickly that he thought he'd imagined it. It blazed a line across the floor in front of him. He looked to see where it had come from, his face the picture of astonishment. Before he could think to ask the how of it, he turned as another stream, this time of water, passed by his peripheral vision. Horus tracked the path of the liquid to the line of fire, which was now out. The cup he held was empty. He swung around to Ari and Martha, sputtering.

"Did you … what was … how?" The thoughts came too quickly for Horus to form words. He finally settled on, "Which one of you did that?" He looked back and forth from Martha to Ari.

"We are not as helpless as we appear," Martha said, confirming Horus' suspicion. She'd had enough of being demure.

Thankfully, the matter was no longer arguable, considering the adults had all come to the same conclusion (after having a talk with Horus). She heard him murmur something about the *neteru*, accompanied by a lot of agitated flapping of his hands. Apparently, he believed the children were heavenly creatures. Martha figured that perhaps, they had made Horus a believer in divine intervention after all. When the adults cast a look in her direction, she tried her best to give what she thought was an enigmatic smile, delivered by an all-powerful, supernatural being. It could only help their cause, she justified.

"We're all leaving now," Horus announced to the children as he returned to their side. He began to lay out the details of their escape. The children hardly understood much of it but trusted that Horus knew what *he* was talking about. He mentioned something about "the way of the sea" as the travel route they would take, whatever that meant. Meanwhile, the Egyptian guide determined that he would take his original charges and hopefully provide a diversion, giving the family time to get away. He didn't much relish the thought of being the hero, but it was rather daring. He could outwit the Roman soldiers, he thought. Probably.

The family would set out first, with the children. Horus would wait a short while, then come behind the family and cover their trail as best he could in the darkness before veering off to take a different path. Hopefully, come daylight, there would be no sign of the direction the family had taken. Horus would not be so careful to cover his own tracks as he went. If the soldiers followed, they should come after him and his employers. Maybe they could still double back to the city and hide within the caravan of camels without attracting much notice and lose themselves among the other travelers. *Yes, it could work*, he thought, nodding in affirmation. Horus almost crowed at the visual – the soldiers would arrive too late. There would be nothing to be done for it but to report back to the king. He would love to be witness to that scene! The king's plan thwarted by such as he; his chest swelled at the very idea.

"They may come looking for us, but we'll be long gone," he concluded, feeling very smart about his plan. "And the best part is no one, not one of the neighbors, will be able to tell them!" He almost smacked his hands together in his glee at outsmarting the king.

"Won't that be dangerous for them?" Martha inquired, seeing a flaw in his plan. But Horus was high, swept up on a wave of euphoria. He blew off her objections.

"They'll be looking for four men – strangers to this country." He shook his head as he said it. "Why harm villagers? We'll be gone; the soldiers can only report that back to the king. End. Of. Story." He fluttered his eyes and annunciated each word, punctuating by overly sounding the last consonant.

"We don't have time for this," Mal said, looking about him. For what, only he knew. "We must be on our way." Ari regarded him carefully, half expecting Mal to start ranting again. He tried to read his troubled friend's face, but Mal averted his eyes. Ari looked to Martha instead, giving her a questioning look. The one she returned was likewise puzzled. Mal seemed fine, for the moment. Ari decided to leave it for the time being.

The children gathered together their meager belongings and prepared to leave. The others were waiting in the outer chamber, split already into two groups. Their benefactors stood to one side, their drawn and sober faces matched by the grave expressions of Yosef and his wife opposite them. All heads turned in the direction of Horus and the children as they entered the room.

"You've been told, yes?" Anil questioned as he drew close to the trio. His brows furrowed, and the anxiety was apparent in his eyes.

"Yes," Ari answered for them all. Mal and Martha nodded in agreement.

"We don't want to leave you here," Anil began, doing his hand wringing thing. "But we feel it best." He fumbled for words to go on. "I am somewhat responsible for you all, as I drew you into this. We all feel, however, that this is the best course of action." He gestured to his fellow travelers and continued, "I, and my companions, will take the burden of the risk, you see. We will act in such a way that if the soldiers come, they will follow *us*." The little man gulped audibly at that, a little in awe of his own bravery. "This should give you all the opportunity to get out of harm's way. It's the least we can do, I feel, being that we have drawn attention to the child and subsequently, may have brought trouble to this family's door." His eyes pleaded with them to understand. He fretted over the young people, despite Horus' testimony as to their miraculous abilities.

Mal stepped forward, so close that the little man had to look up to him. He reached out and put his hand on Anil's shoulder, comforting him.

"We can take care of ourselves," Mal assured the small man. "And, we will watch over the child and make sure he is safe." It was a vow, one Mal intended to see until completion. Ari and Martha resisted the urge to look at each other, choosing instead to back up Mal's statement. Mal's resolve was admirable, notwithstanding the fact that he, only a short time before, was unable to care for himself. But he appeared to be over his episode. Who knew? Perhaps he would not have another. Anil, for his part, was resigned to their course of action, for it was the only way. He considered the matter settled and took Mal at his word. Without further delay, he turned to the couple and the young child, cradled in his mother's arms. Yosef reached for Anil and clasped his hands.

"The LORD bless you and keep you," he began.

"The LORD make his face shine upon you and be gracious to you, "Anil took up the phrase, smiling while noting Yosef's surprise that he would be familiar with the prayer.

"The LORD turn his face toward you and give you peace," Yosef returned his smile and completed the blessing.

"My eyes are blessed to have seen the coming of the King," Sulayman said in his deep, smooth voice. He bowed low and ceremoniously before the family. He straightened, winked at Ari, Mal, and Martha, giving them his big broad smile. To them, he said, "Until we meet again, cousins!"

"Safe travels to us all," Babar added.

"May your God, who has kept us this far, continue to keep us." This last goodbye came from Horus. When all heads turned in his direction, he gave them a look that said, *What?* He sniffed at the group, a trifle indignantly. He had worshipped many gods during his lifetime. But he had never seen things such as what he'd witnessed during this journey. So, he was finding he could have faith in their God, too.

Chapter Seventeen

Julius

… was doing what he did best – tracking. He'd been doing that since he was a small boy. It was a skill taught to him by his father, who was taught by his father before him. Small animals, larger prey, it didn't matter. Ole Jules, as his father often said, could track them all. It was a real source of pride for him. Once he got a nose for something, he had to follow it through. And something, *someone*, had garnered his full attention.

Julius had seen the children in the marketplace, although he pretended not to. He had noted the group they'd joined and the direction for which they'd set out. And now, he was on their trail. He'd waited just long enough to avoid arousing suspicion among his fellow officers (no need to involve them), hung back just far enough to avoid detection by Ari and his companions. But he was on them. Jules had watched them, surreptitiously, all afternoon. He knew the town where they were headed. The only question was, why? What did they hope to find there? And what business did Ari and his friends have with the men who'd visited the palace? For what cause had they formed an alliance?

Ole Jules was a curious cat. Sometimes too much for his own good, he admitted. But he pursued them nonetheless.

****

Herod

... was disturbed. More than just mentally, as was generally thought. His mood was as the workers in his palace had never seen - beyond irrational and blathering on about a child. A child, for goodness sake! What child was this that could interrupt his slumber and haunt his waking hours, too? To bring unrest to a royal court already in constant uproar was not a good thing for its inhabitants. The king,

175

difficult on his best days, was unbalanced and given to fits of fury. His workers trembled at every rise and fall of his voice, in anticipation of his next act. They were already well aware of his poor impulse control.

Truly, the four could've traveled to Beth Lechem and returned ten times by now, he seethed inwardly. It was only a short distance up the road. Would they dare disobey a king and agent of the Roman government, in his very region? He would rain down his wrath upon them all - man, woman, and child - for their audacity. He had been given authority over all of Judea and had the full support and backing of Caesar. They would not have the nerve to disobey his order.

But even as these thoughts crossed his mind, he knew the magi had done just that. Fury contorted his features into an ugly mask, fearful to behold. The wise men and their guide would not return this way. He could see it now, as he did not then, recalling their demeanor towards him. He read, in hindsight, their intention to thwart his plan.

Unseen by all, stood the Strange Man, working the king up to a fever pitch. None knew the insinuations of a kingdom lost that the Strange Man whispered in the king's ear. A legacy that could never be regained by Herod or his descendents because of the birth of this *one child*. The thought wormed around in the ruler's head, seeking purchase until it found a foothold. A picture of his future was revealed, of him and his family being ousted and put on the run. Or worse yet, put to death. He was, by turns, frightened and furious until he nearly vibrated from the force of his emotions. Perspiration ran down the king's back, beads of the salty liquid peppered his face. He shook with the effort of trying to rein himself.

Why? The voice whispered, encouragingly, suggestively, silken and caressing. *Why hold back? Are you not King? Why not just let … go?*

"AAAARGH!" Like a dam bursting suddenly, the king let loose a vitriolic spewing of such language that left those unfortunate enough to be in close proximity cowering in fear. His eyes rolled about in his head, and he practically lathered about his mouth.

"GUARD!" The king roared at no one in particular. He expected obedience, immediately, no matter the order. Sure enough, a young guard appeared, at his command. Despite his youth, he seemed stoic enough – that is, he didn't quiver as the king bellowed. Perhaps his appearance was misleading, and the soldier was already battle hardened, for he didn't blink at the king's (nor the king's quarters) state of disarray. He looked straight ahead, his body erect as he waited for the king's edict.

****

Erasmus

... was a lout. A brute, even. He knew that, gloried in it, even. Someone had to do the work others found distasteful, so he routinely volunteered for assignments that might cause others to shirk. He was proud to be that one his superiors called on at such times, for he excelled in this area. It was a unique skill set, really. One that only the most hardened and ambitious soldiers displayed, he told himself. Surely, the title of *centurion* was in his future if he just stayed the course. And who knew what rank he could achieve after that?

Unlike the "tender" Jules with his *feelings*, Erasmus reveled in duties that made others squeamish. And just where was Julius anyway? As their scout, he should have been right here in the thick of it. But he had no appetite for such deeds and would get out of them whenever possible. Still, somehow, Jules was a favored pet among the officers; a likable person.

Erasmus, however, was a different sort, altogether. He relished the thought of getting his hands dirty, and this opportunity to shine before his superiors was not lost on him. He reasoned within himself, no task could be too much for him. Nothing would turn his stomach; no deed too vile. He wouldn't let it. This was his chance to get ahead and, even surpass Julius. Erasmus wanted to be more than just a tool to be used. He would become a machine, a machine *of war*, to be exact. Give him an order, and he intended to churn it out and follow it with such precision that it would surely impress.

Which was why, when given the assignment, although he knew it would require a certain amount of brutality, Erasmus was not dissuaded. He had a duty to perform. The palace was in upheaval; the king was unsettled. Erasmus could bring order, with his actions. Save the day, so to speak. He had an assignment, and he would carry it out, simple as that. To that end, he was given a small unit; a larger contingent was not needed for this *mean* responsibility. Those involved were insignificant, their lives a mere vapor.

Erasmus chose his accomplices carefully, for this was his time to shine. Those who were like Julius (soft, that is), he discarded as unworthy. He needed more heartless individuals like himself, bent only on obeying the will of the king, as issued via their commander. Their given mission: to crush, kill, and destroy innocence.

Chapter Eighteen

Though the sky was still dark and the night cool, to their dismay, certain villagers were already stirring. Early risers, Ari thought, wondering what this new development could do for their chances to leave discreetly. The party debated the idea of who should leave first, so as not to draw unnecessary attention. In the end, they simply decided to leave together while they still had cover of darkness, in as inconspicuous a fashion possible (given the size of their company). But they had to go. They could delay no longer. It didn't matter who left first anymore; they all had to leave, and quickly, for time was running out. Haste was of utmost importance, for the king could discover their ruse at any moment. Soldiers could be in pursuit, even now.

With luck, Horus hoped, any neighbors who had seen them could not speculate on their whereabouts, even were they so inclined. *It shouldn't be so difficult,* he figured. They had arrived after most of the town had retired – what could the inhabitants of the town have *seen* enough to testify? He gave a mental shrug. The way Horus saw it, the villagers couldn't tell what they didn't know.

Mal seemed calm enough for the most part; far as Ari could tell, Mal was almost normal. But Ari could see the sheen of sweat on his face in the moonlight, which was slowly giving way to the morning. Day was breaking and the trio, along with the young mother, father, and child, had to put some distance between themselves and the (mostly) sleeping village.

****

Julius was mad. It was a small thing, a minute detail, but something that would not escape the attention of a tracker like him. Ari and company were trying to cover their trail – but for what reason? And, they'd bungled the job in their attempt. That's what enraged him. Ineptitude! And who was pursuing them? They were on the run – the signs were all there. The warm remains of a cooking fire and quickly cooling lamps were indicators that they'd only recently vacated the home. But where to and why?

Julius would leave that mystery to be resolved once he'd caught up with them, which shouldn't be long. He'd only delayed his arrival out of curiosity as to what they were about. But this, this botched attempt to hide their goings on was unforgivable, as far as he was concerned. He made a mental note to make sure *his* son had better skills of concealment. Who knew what trouble he'd find himself in? He paused at that and became suddenly alert, standing straight and still. His head cocked to one side as a sensation, warm and tingly, passed over his body. Julius knew then, just in thinking those very words, that they would come to pass.

The moment passed, and Julius gave himself a mental shake to clear his thoughts. Why dwell on a future that had yet to materialize? He wasn't even married, and no wife was in sight. He threw a broken leaf down in mock disgust and promised himself that he would teach Ari and his friends when he saw them again. He thought more tenderly of the lad, now that he'd realized that Ari may have not had anyone to instruct him in such things. It further firmed his resolve to pass on his knowledge to his son even sooner – from the crib, if he were able!

He shook his head slowly and smiled ruefully to himself as he viewed other signs that a party had recently passed by. It was there, in the broken grass, disturbed dirt and sand and overturned rocks. Now that he'd cooled down and given it some thought, it was as if they had *not* tried to disguise their trail, but advertised it instead. A child could find them in the dark. At least four, he surmised, passed this way. A small one, perhaps the little girl he'd seen them with earlier, and Ari and the bigger boy could account for two others. But who was the fourth? And how or why had he been included in their group?

He'd get answers soon enough, he knew, as he turned to follow their trail. And, he'd make sure that when he caught up with them, Ari and his companions would know what NOT to do next time they were on the run.

Chapter Nineteen

"How did you know what to do?" Martha asked of Ari. She was coming to find that Ari was multifaceted in his talents. The question was two-fold.

They had parted company with Horus and his charges, the two groups going in different directions, soon after leaving the house of Yosef. Ari was carrying precious cargo, for the little boy had suddenly reached for Ari, wanting to be carried. Although there was a mule for the family's hastily gathered belongings and the boy could have ridden on top, Ari had obliged, feeling drawn to the little one. Smaller children seemed to like him, he acknowledged; he'd mainly experienced problems with those of his age group. The little one laid his head, trustingly, on Ari's shoulder for a moment, then perked up and looked eagerly around him. His eyes were too alert, taking in his surroundings. He should have been sleeping, Ari thought. It was too early in the morning (really, too late at night) – just his luck to have such an alert toddler on his hands.

As they were departing the small town, they'd encountered a beggar lying across the entrance. Ari had nearly stumbled across his prone figure and smothered his yelp of surprise in the darkness. The little one was jostled when Ari lost his footing for a moment, but he didn't cry out. He seemed to know intuitively he should be quiet. But he did reach out his hand as if he could balance them both with such an action. His eyes, now become so familiar to Ari, gave him a look that plainly said, *whoa*!

The beggar was awakened by the pressure of Ari's hard sandal upon his leg. He had fallen asleep, exhausted, after a day of attempting to find work (useless, he knew, because of his deformity) and foraging for what food he could find. It had been a particularly hard day, and he had fallen asleep, unthinkingly, across the entrance to the little hamlet.

Now, someone had come to disturb his slumber. He sat up and viewed the group with owlish eyes, trying to pierce the darkness to see just who had nearly trampled him. He saw an attractive young man, holding a little boy. The beggar pulled himself and his rags together, folding his legs as best he could under himself in an attempt to make himself smaller and get out of their way. His manner was apologetic as if he were used to being trampled upon and treated as if he did not matter. His bare feet were especially pitiful to Ari, as they signaled that the wretched man didn't own the meanest of comforts, even a pair of sandals.

The little boy, though, continued to stretch his hand out toward the beggar, reaching for him. The beggar, smiled in reply, lifting a gnarled, twisted hand in their direction and smiling at the toddler. He loved children, even as much as he was allowed to be around them. They, at least, did not judge or abuse him.

Ari was moved to compassion as he viewed the malformed limb. He wished he could do ... *something* to ease the man's condition. But what? He had no money. Ari followed the example of the toddler, thinking to offer solace if naught else. He reached for the beggar, too – noting that the withered hand looked dry, even in the moonlight. Parched, he thought, and in need of moisture. The beggar's hand reminded Ari of his own finger when he'd unwittingly drained it of too much fluid. Hmmm, he wondered. *Maybe*. It definitely wouldn't hurt to try.

His hand met that of the beggar, joining it in the dim light. And the moment Ari touched that palsied hand, he felt something stir in him. It beckoned to the gift in him. Power stirred within, seeking release. It flowed out and into the poor beggar, and Ari was unable to let go.

His body gave a jolt and Ari felt, rather than saw, the current flowing between him and the beggar. But he knew by the man's reaction that he'd felt it too. Instinctively, Ari called to water in the afflicted body, visualizing and demanding that the hidden pools of liquid from the deep recesses of that deformed body be released. *Flood this limb*, Ari found himself praying, fervently. Fill it, restore it, he commanded, instinctively. In awe, he and the beggar watched as bodily fluids redistributed throughout the defective hand, plumping and filling in the previously dry spaces. Fingers wiggled, then threaded Ari's own; the man gave them a squeeze to verify they were fully functional.

The beggar thrust his perfect hand, now bound with Ari's upward into the dawning sky, victoriously. Joy, relief and a myriad of emotions flooded his face. He couldn't believe his good fortune. And Ari, even though he'd been instrumental in the feat, was dumbstruck. His face reflected his complete and utter astonishment. A miracle! He had just wrought a genuine miracle.

The beggar obviously agreed with Ari for he began to rejoice. A whoop escaped his frail frame, and Ari found, the beggar was merely crippled, not dumb. Fearful that his antics would draw unwanted attention, the beggar was quickly shushed by Ari. The little one, still held fast in Ari's arms, caught on to the game quickly. He put a tiny finger to his lips.

"Shhhh …" he mouthed.

The beggar barely managed to quiet his verbal exultation as he gleefully gathered his scant belongings. He couldn't entirely refrain from making happy grunts all the while. Ari was ecstatic for the fellow, but now he was causing a tiny disruption and was beyond restraining. Ari looked to his traveling companions; Yosef and his wife, Martha, and Mal, his expression a mixture of awe and disbelief. He hardly knew what to think of what had just happened. He had no explanation. Ari had just followed through on a … *hunch*. And now he had a formerly disabled man on his hands who couldn't stop praising.

"Yah! He is a healer! Adonai is a deliverer!" he cried jubilantly. The beggar had tried to whisper. He really did, but he just couldn't contain the exultation over his deliverance. No sooner than he would calm himself, the thought of what had just happened would cause an "OH!" to burst forth, and he would start up again. The man did a little shuffling dance on the road. Ari batted his hands in the air, using a downward motion to try to further restrain the man. But such a feeling could not be contained. There were tears in the beggar's eyes, and he proclaimed, "I have been rescued from my despair!"

Ari empathized with the man, but they didn't have time for this. It was inconvenient, for sure. But looking into the face of the beggar, his face shining with effusive praise, Ari knew he wouldn't exchange their encounter for the entire world. Still, he had to tamp down the fellow's exuberance. He finally grabbed the man with his free hand and gave him a little shake to get his attention. Now that he was standing, Ari noticed the beggar was quite small. Ari, being much taller, leaned into him, whispering earnestly:

"Please! You must stop this!" He looked intently into the beggar's eyes, his frustration with the situation evident. Ari cast furtive glances about them. He hoped no one had heard the laudations of the beggar and that the fellow had not drawn attention to their imminent departure (though it was hard to imagine he had not). At last, the man calmed. "What is your name?" Ari asked him.

"My name?" The beggar regarded Ari, and a wondrous expression passed his features. No one had bothered to address him by any formal name in so long; he'd felt it hardly mattered. But now, here stood a young man, clearly a messenger sent by the Lord to save him from his distress, inquiring of his name. Asking for *his* name! It was like the encounter of his forefather, Ya'akov, when his name was changed to *Yisra'el*.

"Micah," he bobbed his head as he said it, as if in agreement. Yes, that was – IS his name. "My name is Micah." Perhaps the angel would change his name now. He went to fall on his knees then, realizing that he was addressing an emissary of the Most High. Micah bowed low to the ground.

"No, noooo," Ari looked about himself again, uncomfortably. "None of that," and lifted the man to his feet. "I need – *we need* your help." It had only occurred to him, just then, that they needed to take another course of action now that their carefully planned escape had been foiled. No doubt, most of the village remained asleep, but who knew how much the ruckus had disturbed their slumber? Better to put this fellow, Micah, to good use and keep him busy, but most importantly, QUIET.

Micah looked back at Ari, questioningly, eager to serve.

Ari looked around. *Ah*, he thought when his eyes fell on a long, leafy branch. It was just what was needed. Ari handed the toddler off to Martha quite abruptly. He walked over to the branch, picked it up and handed it over to Micah, placing it into his restored appendage. The man held up the branch for inspection, viewing it curiously, but got distracted again by the miracle that was his hand. Micah hadn't held anything in that hand for years, though he'd never been able to use it properly. He began to wave the branch, back and forth, his upturned face rapturous.

"Yes, yes … just like that," Ari deliberately misunderstood and redirected the man's waving motions towards the ground. "Yes, just like that," the man's hand's made sweeping motions across the ground, making patterns in the sand. He became engrossed in his task and went about it diligently, scraping over all of the area around them. Whilst Micah was otherwise engaged, Ari stepped past him and went over to his traveling companions. Mal and Martha were still wide-eyed, but he'd noticed that the husband and wife didn't seem overly perturbed by the events they'd just witnessed.

"He can help us," Ari spoke in low tones to the group. He gestured to the man, who was happily preoccupied with his task. "Micah can–" Ari broke off and moved suddenly to the man's side. "No, not there," and redirected the man over to their side of the road once more. Ari rejoined the others.

"What are you saying, Ari?" Martha was without an inkling as to what Ari intended, and that was saying something. She considered herself to be most perceptive, easily picking up on even adult things, but especially so amongst those of her own age. Their deliberations were usually simpler in nature. But this time, she just didn't get it. She waited for him to elaborate, somewhat impatiently, her features expectant.

"He can help hide the direction we're taking," Ari said. To him, the solution was obvious, and he felt a little smug because he knew something she did not. He resisted the urge to roll his eyes and taunt Martha. But he didn't have time to get her riled up. He looked pointedly at the long branch that Micah was painting the ground with in sweeping motions. Martha's eyebrows shot up to her hairline, and her mouth formed an oval. Ari could tell the pieces had fallen into place.

Ari had suddenly seen the flaw in Horus' great diversionary tactic. There would still be two sets of footprints to betray that two different groups of people left *Beth Lechem* that night. His group needed more cover. He went over to the beggar, taking his hands, once again, to gain his attention.

"Here's what I need you to do."

****

Ari had the beggar follow them out of the city limits, sweeping all the way and obscuring their tracks. Micah followed them obediently as he dragged the branch behind him. His eyes remained on Ari more often than not, his devotion unquestioned. As the day began to dawn, chasing away the last vestiges of the night sky, Ari turned to the beggar.

"I need you to go back."

At this, Micah's face became puzzled. Back? He'd thought Ari was leading him on a grand adventure. There was not much reason for him to go back – no family, no wife. Go back? For what? Ari correctly guessed his thoughts and answered.

"I need you to go back, dragging the branch, to hide even your tracks." He looked at the man directly, trying to convey urgency. "They can't find us. This is important." More bewilderment on Micah's features. Again, with the *why*. And confusion over who "they" were. "I don't have time to explain, Micah. Do this, for *me*." Ari hoped he'd earned enough loyalty to ask the man to go back to the village and cover for them, if necessary. He was pretty sure of it, but he tacked on extra insurance just in case. "For them," Ari motioned to the couple just ahead of them and nodded down at the toddler, now sleeping peacefully in his arms. Micah looked at him sadly.

"I don't want to leave you – I know you must be a messenger of the Lord." When Micah spoke, his voice was a bit rusty, but it was filled with reverence. He hadn't spoken for much of their time together, preferring to hum his songs of praise. His eyes touched on the little boy, slumbering and unaware of their peril. But Micah knew. He just didn't understand why a child and his family could be in danger. However, Micah was obedient, if nothing else, to the young man he regarded now as master. "I want to stay with you, with him." Micah touched the child. Ari just shook his head in response. "But where can I go?"

"Back to the village. Cover your tracks on the way back," said Ari. "Even if they see you coming back, they'll only see a man dragging a branch and think nothing of it." It occurred to Ari just then, and his face lit up, "They may not even recognize you!"

Indeed, Micah had undergone a transformation. No longer bent and feeble in his gait, he now stood strong and confident, growing more so with each step that he took. Even his rags had been exchanged for a clean garment, supplied by Martha, who was happy to shed the clothing that Anil had given her. Micah had stared at her in amazement, seeing then that she was a girl. But so far, it was not the strangest thing he had seen. He was now a different man because of the intervention of these … heavenly beings. And he knew Ari's plan could work. It made sense. Still he tried one more time.

"Can I not go with you further?" he pleaded, "I can help." He *could* help. He knew it. He was no longer debilitated – his hand was like new. He demonstrated by dropping the branch and holding his hand up for Ari to view.

"You would be helping by going back, Micah," said Ari. He spoke quietly to soften the words. "Just in a different way." It wasn't rejection, but to Micah, it may have seemed as such.

Micah sighed and nodded his head in acquiescence. There was wisdom in what the young man said. It was a good idea. Still, Micah was sorrowful as he turned to go and headed back to *Beth Lechem*. But his desire to help those who had given him aid weighed heavily upon his heart. He gave them all one last encompassing look, then picked up his branch and pulled it behind him as he went in the opposite direction. Dejected, he tried hard not to drag his feet, too.

****

Julius traced their steps, stalking his prey for a short while before an obvious thought occurred to him. What if this trail was made so extremely visible just to trick anyone who came after them? Julius halted. The more he thought about it, the more he became convinced that he had been duped. He had underestimated Ari.

He smiled a little, at that, feeling unaccountably proud. His boy – erm, Ari, he meant – actually turned out to be quite astute. To fool a seasoned tracker like himself – his chest swelled at the thought, but he attributed that to his breathing. Jules took another deep breath to dispel that illogical feeling. His chest expanded again, but there was no accompanying sense of pride this time. In any case, it appeared that this Ari was already someone to be reckoned with. Maybe they *were* related somehow. Whatever the case, Julius knew then that when he did have a son, he would want him to be as resourceful as Ari.

Chapter Twenty

"I guess I knew because I had been toying with my gift earlier," Ari finally responded to Martha's query. After sending Micah on his way, he'd taken up his place among the group, once again. "I knew that I could call the water under my skin and shift it where I wanted it to go." He gave an it-was-nothing shrug, "That's what I did with Micah. I don't know why but just suddenly *felt* I could."

Ari felt sure this was the incident Martha was talking about but, he had experienced something else, simultaneously, along with this miracle. An event that Ari felt was wondrous in its own right. When Martha still looked askance at Ari, he realized that she was asking him about that, too. She gave him a bug-eyed look to indicate he should continue.

"Oh, that!" He smiled his wry smile. "Doesn't everybody do that?" he said jokingly, before replying more soberly

"When I saw the branch, it brought to mind my father teaching me about tracking prey and how to avoid being traced myself. He said, 'One day you may not want to be found.' Funny how I didn't remember it until just then." Ari's eyes took on a faraway look as he ruminated. He recalled how he was suddenly aware of the knowledge while at the same time feeling it had not always been there.

Ari's mind had been flooded with images out of nowhere, of sessions spent with his father following the trails of animals and people. And disguising his trail, Ari now realized. The recollections were still coming to him now – as if he were only now being made aware of their purpose. His training suddenly made sense, as if his father had prepared him for just this contingency. But how could his father have known this need would arise?

****

Mal trod the road before him, keeping tempo with the steps of the mule, which now carried the little boy. What was his name? He couldn't even think of it, for the mother kept referring to him as her "little lamb." It was plain to see she adored her child, and Mal could understand why. He invoked in Mal a desire to protect him, and blind devotion. Mal didn't understand why. He didn't bother to try, though. Somehow, his headache was kept at bay, the closer he stayed to the little boy. The voices were quiet now. Mal was just glad for peace. Yosef and his wife seemed content for the time being to let Mal take the lead reins of the mule as the action seemed to calm him. But the couple kept watch over Mal as he shadowed their son and stayed within arm's reach. Yosef's hand was on the beast for a steadying influence while Miriam kept her hand on her son's leg. A precautionary measure, to be sure, for they knew little of young Mal. They both felt assured that he was on their side, though. He seemed determined to help their flight from those that sought to harm them.

Ari and Martha followed behind, just a few paces. They had traveled yet another endless mile, she guessed, though there was no way to be certain. This road was indistinguishable from any other, dipping and rising with the hilly landscape. It was lined on either side with trees, trees, and yet more, trees. At intervals, she saw olive groves, whose fruit she longed to sample, which only served to remind her that she was hungry. They passed flocks of sheep, overseen by watchful shepherds, which called to mind their friend, David. Usually, Martha enjoyed the beauty of such scenery, even though it was somewhat familiar to her, simply because it was a change from the fishing harbor near where she lived. But she felt like she was waiting for something to happen, and it was making her restless.

At least on the major roads, she would have some break from the monotony provided by the stone pillars that dotted the highway at intervals. (She'd recalled seeing the markers on journeys she'd taken with her family. When asked, her father had then explained their purpose: to count down the number of miles left to reach the great city of Rome.) This system had been put in place well before her time. On this road, however, there were no such markers to indicate the passing of miles. But Yosef seemed to be well acquainted with the path.

All she could gather of their journey was that they were traveling west, for the rising sun was at their backs. She noticed that the terrain changed subtly as they went. Dirt gave way to sand, in places. That was of little interest to her, though. She lived near sand. For lack of something better to do, she committed herself to watch Mal with keen eyes. Martha was determined to miss nothing (just as she had not missed what had happened earlier with

Ari). Curiosity drove her conversation with Ari while concern fueled her observation of Mal. So far, no more fits of apoplexy marred their journey. It was as if the last incident had never occurred.

But Mal was far from fine. He tried to put on a good face, but in truth, his strength was fading fast. By now, the sun had risen and was at his back. He grew warm from exertion and the added heat only served to further sap his energy. He removed his outer garment in an effort to cool himself, but it didn't help much. Soon, perspiration had the tunic sticking to his body. His legs felt weighed down, and his leaden footsteps dragged from just the effort of putting one in front of the other. He lagged farther and farther behind until Yosef took the reins, purportedly to give Mal a break, but also out of concern for Mal and the child.

Wordlessly, Martha went to his side. Ari took him up on the other side, slipping his arm under Mal's, and lending his strength. Mal gave

Martha a feeble look – why was his strength flagging so? He felt helpless. And, his headache, that unbearable pounding, had returned.

Chapter Twenty-One

Julius had left *Beth Lechem* far behind. He went after Ari and his friends with dogged determination. Ole Jules, he'd heard his father say time and again, was not one to give up easily. Julius always tried hard to live up to those words.

He'd followed a trail that was just lines really; it looked like something he would do to disguise his footsteps when he was a young boy, as his father had taught him. It was rudimentary, at best, and he supposed, would do in a pinch. Maybe Ari had felt a pinch, which made Julius smile. Better than nothing, he thought and continued to follow a trail that was quickly becoming lost in the swirling patterns of dirt and sand created by ever increasing gusts of wind. *It was certainly blustery out today,* Jules thought, as he pushed against the strong breeze.

At the sound of someone's approach, Julius stepped to the side of the road and hid behind the trunk of a tree. He needn't have bothered, he realized, at the appearance of the crestfallen small man. Julius doubted the wandering undersized figure would have noticed had he been standing in the middle of the path, so downcast was his demeanor. But oh! The little fellow held a clue in his hand – a long branch that he dragged along the ground behind him, concealing his tracks as he went. Julius knew then he was that much closer to catching up with Ari and company. He broke into a jog, eager to be on the hunt.

****

Erasmus sneered as he left *Beth Lechem* and returned to *Yerushalaim*. Fool! Did they take him for a fool? He was certain they knew more than they were telling. Well, they would live to regret it (he'd seen to that).

And that stupid *elder* of the town or whatever he was. He thought he could stop them – reason with Erasmus and his men – have them go against the king's orders! He'd shown them. All of them. He was no one to be trifled with.

In the end, the self-proclaimed head of the town, Shammah, had told all he'd known, with little initiation on the part of the lead soldier. Erasmus knew the sort; Shammah wanted a title, needed to be in charge; he was an authority seeker. He'd approached the soldiers as they'd entered the village, volunteering information they hadn't even asked to appear as if he were on their level. As if he had the authority to speak for the entire village.

"There was a group of strangers that entered the village after nightfall," he offered, helpfully. "You must be looking for them – they went to Yosef's place but left during the night." He indicated a rough home towards the far end of town. "My wife and I saw them as they came in. She sat playing with our son, Hiram, near the window, so I noticed them as they walked by." Shammah was most talkative, to be sure and was determined to be the one in the know. And, he was just as determined to pass on that knowledge.

"I figured they were up to no good," he whispered conspiratorially, smiling foolishly at Erasmus.

"Well," Erasmus finally answered, "You'll wish you had detained them." He dismounted from his horse and unsheathed his sword. "Our orders were to bring the death of a child." His eyes scanned the onlookers and rested on Shammah's wife and babe. The village leader's eyes widened in alarm as Erasmus' meaning became clear.

"He didn't say which …"

****

Mal fell to his knees, unable to go on. He'd tried, but his body was in distress; trembling limbs, overly salivating mouth, wild eyes that overcame his ability to continue. He'd given in to it, fighting against it was too much. The voices were back again. The loud roar filled his head.

"AGH!" His head felt like it would split open. Not again. He couldn't take much more of this. Screaming. Running. Chaos. Babies – no! Not the babies! He was there again, only this time, he knew where *there* was: that little town, *Beth Lechem*. A saying, a reading from the holy writings, forced from the hindermost part of his mind; emblazed on the fore: *Lamentation and bitter weeping, Rachel weeping for her children, and would not be comforted, because they are not.*

The images and voices whirled in his head until he could not tell nightmare from reality. Pain that was so unimaginable, tears ran from his eyes. Rivers of water flowed until the pain was no longer because Mal was no longer. His eyes stared up at the sky unblinkingly, glazed over. He was lost to his companions. His mind was caught up in a maelstrom of terror.

****

Julius was a little stumped. Not about the direction the children had taken. He'd already figured that out and was hot on their trail. He expected he'd catch up with them soon. He had taken his time, deliberating what to do with them once he'd found them. Now, he feared he may have squandered his opportunity. Something was wrong – very, VERY wrong. Rumors reached him, carried to him on the foul wind, of a massacre. Unfortunately, Jules knew well the stench of blood, the sounds of war and death. It was behind him, he was sure, but he didn't want to turn back and find out for certain. He didn't want to know, he really didn't. Just the visions that were conjured up by the echoes – sharp swords being drawn, cries of alarm, faint and weakened by the distance – were enough to compel him to stop.

He closed his eyes, strained his ears, feeling a little sickened. Bloody business was at work; he knew, by the *sching* of metal, the sound of a weapon being pulled from its scabbard. But there was no accompanying clashing sound of battle, metal meeting metal. He imagined, rather than heard, the slicing of flesh as the sword came down. He knew what was happening. The Roman war machine had been set in motion, Caesar's brand of keeping the peace. He had no stomach for it. But why? What had the sleeping settlement he'd just left done? How could they have possibly offended the powers that be in such a way so as to deserve this swift retribution? It had been mere hours since he'd left *Yerushalaim*. The order had been issued and carried out swiftly.

At times like this, he truly hated being a soldier. The only comfort remaining to him was that he had not taken part in the judgment they had delivered. But even this was not the cause for his bewilderment. As the echoes of destruction decreased, another reached his ears; a portent of evil, foretelling a certain end. The thud of hooves falling, striking the rock and packed earth, pierced his consciousness. The sun had climbed further up in the sky. It was full on daylight now. He turned back and squinted at the bright light, wondering just how much time he had. And what did any of this have to do with Ari and his friends? Julius knew he wouldn't be the only one to catch up to them soon.

He strained his ears toward the sound. Yes. YES! The hoof beats were fading away into the distance, away from him, going in the opposite direction. A sigh of relief escaped him. Julius had been given a reprieve, but he didn't know for how long. He prayed it was enough time to reach Ari.

****

Shortly after Erasmus arrived in *Yerushalaim*, but just before he would make his report to his commander, he began to have second thoughts. Not because he had done anything he'd regretted, just that he'd not done enough. His misgiving plagued him as he drew near the stable, dismounted and was about to tether his horse. He halted in the middle of the action as his internal debate waged on:

"Maybe you didn't get him," the voice argued.

"I did," he crowed to the voice, "I got them all! Not one was left."

"BUT … you don't know that he was even there still … the child … maybe he has escaped!" The voice said, silky in its insistence.

"I – I," Erasmus wavered, not as certain as he was only moments before. "I know I did …" his voice trailed off. He was speaking aloud now. His companions looked questioningly at him. "I did!"

"Huh? What're you talkin' 'bout Ras?" Alópéx queried. The Fox had been reinstated amongst their ranks, on the condition that he redeem himself with this assignment. He wanted to do just that, so he had not shirked at the horrendous act that left them all covered in blood. Some men snapped under such pressure but not him. And certainly, he would wager, not Erasmus. They were two of a kind, ambitious for advancement and equal to whatever came, usually. But the look he gave Erasmus was reserved for one deranged. Had he already been driven mad?

"He lives ... he lives ... he lives ... you have failed!" the voice was chanting now, determined not to be ignored.

Erasmus gathered the reins in his hands and got back on the pale horse. Alópéx's eyes bugged. What was Erasmus *doing*?

"I just want to be sure," he said to the wide-eyed Alópéx. "We're going back." There were a few grumbles, but the regiment followed Erasmus' example and mounted their steeds once more.

****

Mal lay face down in the dirt, overwhelmed by the enormity of his emotions. He clawed at ground about him, unable to withstand all he had seen and heard. Mal rolled over on his back, rocking from side to side on the ground in utter misery. He tried covering his ears, and by turns, his eyes in an attempt to block the auditory and visual assault on his senses. Martha rubbed his back in an attempt to comfort him, but Mal would not be comforted. The images tormented him and were engraved on the backs of his eyelids, it seemed to him. He could not get away from them.

Ari looked helplessly on the fallen Mal. He was strongest of them and the oldest – if he could not withstand this trial, how could they (Ari and Martha, that is) be expected to hold out? Ari wondered what this could mean for him and Martha. Was this a precursor of the test to come for them all? At that moment, Martha met his eyes. He knew she was thinking the same thing. His anxiety was mirrored on her features – fear for Mal and them all.

Martha took charge. Maybe they couldn't fight this – whatever it was – that was wrong with Mal. She felt it had to do with his gift but didn't know how to help. She resolved to do what she could. She took Mal's hand in one of hers, and with the other tried to lift his head to meet her gaze. Perhaps he would recognize her, his cousin, and return to them. Mal resisted her efforts, so she called his name.

"Mal ... Mal ... Mal," she implored of him, and then looked to Ari for help. He answered her with a shrug; his uplifted hands emphasized the gesture. It wasn't uncaring, she knew. Ari just hadn't any idea how he could alleviate Mal's condition.

"What is he saying?" Yosef asked, leaning over the troubled young man. He craned his ear

223

towards Mal, who was now mumbling. Martha paused to listen and then, shook her head. She couldn't make sense of it.

"Something about Rachel," she picked out as much as she could decipher. "Children ... crying?" She gave them all a puzzled look. But none of them seemed to know what it meant either.

"I could hit him on the head," Ari offered, helpfully. Martha glared at him. The look she gave him said that she wanted to hit him on the head. He gave her a sheepish grin, for he only wanted to lighten the mood and take away – even for a moment – the lines of concern etched on her face. That didn't work, he saw, as a moan claimed her attention and she turned back to Mal. Ari did not understand the grave nature of their circumstances, Martha brooded. Without a sober and well Mal, how could they expect to get back? Although Ari might find himself content to pal around with a younger version of his father, she was not so inclined. She

224

wanted to go back home, or at the very least, have the option available to her.

"There, there," she crooned softly to Mal as she stroked his hair, not knowing what else to do. At his ramblings, she just continued to rub his back and arms, hoping to bring some relief. Martha nodded when he looked up, so he could see her commiseration. But, other than an isolated word or two, she couldn't decipher much of what he was trying to communicate.

****

Jules pressed himself, breathing heavily now. He'd cast his armor aside a while back, stowing it under a rock near a tree. He couldn't keep his current pace while wearing it – too heavy. Too hot. He didn't know if he was so heated because of the sun or because he was out and out running now. He supposed it could be a mixture of the two.

But why was it so tiring? As a soldier of the infamous Roman Legion, his body had been subjected to hard training and should be conditioned to such pummeling. Had it been so long since he had required it of himself? Maybe he had gone soft. His limbs felt weighed down.

No matter the why of it, he had to pull himself together. Time could be running out for Ari. He had to reach him, warn him. Jules was stretched to his physical limit, so he stopped to catch his breath, bending over and resting his hands on his knees. He felt a little like throwing up now. But there was no time for that.

He allowed himself a few moments of breathing, knowing that he had to give that much to himself, or he'd give out altogether. In ... and out. In and out. One more. He straightened his torso, gathered his strength (and his resolve). His chest rose and expanded with the effort, pulling in air with great gulps. He had to press on. He didn't even know why. He could not care what happened to Ari and his friends, could he? Nevertheless, he started out again, this time at a slower pace. Still, it was faster than a walk. Jules was determined to reach this young man who bore his features, not even wanting to think of what could happen if he didn't, and finding that he did care.

Chapter Twenty-Two

Frothing unnaturally at the mouth, Erasmus' horse was being pushed beyond endurance. His master, however, did not look to the comfort of the gelding he rode but continued to push the animal. He dug his heels into the horse's side, urging him to go further, faster. He saw the village rising before him again and gave no care that its occupants were in mourning. After the devastation his last visit had brought, he'd think they would flee before him and his men. Yet, they stood before him in the square, not running. Listless and mute, they stared back at him in accusation. They should have more fear.

But like Erasmus, the residents were beyond caring. They railed within, how could he take more? They had been deprived of the life of their village. For some, he had already destroyed that which was most precious. He had taken their very future. They were numb and in shock. Shammah glowered at the soldiers as they passed, as much as he dared, his eyes red and swollen with grief. He didn't worry about what more the soldiers could do to them for the worst thing imaginable had already come upon them all.

That was until Erasmus suddenly wheeled his horse around and came to a halt. His men were forced to draw back their mounts so abruptly that some of the beasts reared back, accompanied by loud snorts of protest. A thought had occurred to Erasmus as he was about to pass the village. Why should he go chasing about to find the little prince? Better to have one here to point the way. As he dismounted, the bereaved mothers wailed at the sight of him, seeing him as the monster they knew him to be.

Erasmus paid their cries no more heed than one would give a flea. Stalking over to the leader of the settlement, he grabbed Shammah up roughly, giving him a shake. Shammah looked back at the head soldier from angry eyes that appeared to be bleeding in their sorrow. *Why hadn't he fought harder?* The guilt ate at Shammah's gut. He'd let them take the life of his son. He, himself, should be dead. He'd failed his family. But he would not let them down again. He stared back at Erasmus, now defiant.

"Tell me where they have gone," Erasmus growled at him. But Shammah made a negative motion with his head. Incapable of speech, he knew he could not lend aid to these barbarians. No! No, he would not be a part of them doing more harm. Erasmus scowled and leaned further in, so close that barely a hairsbreadth separated their faces. "You will tell me," he threatened.

"No!" Shammah shouted defiantly into the face of his enemy. The village leader had found his voice and his strength. "What more can you do to me?" He cried, "You have already taken that which was most precious to me." Shammah sobbed brokenly, looking upon the bloody bundle his wife clutched to her breast. "You have done enough."

"Oh, really?" Erasmus responded calmly, with a speculative gleam in his eyes. That voice was back. *You've not taken all ...* Erasmus nodded in agreement with the voice. He'd caught the look of shared sorrow between Shammah and his wife. Erasmus knew then that he had not taken all that was precious to Shammah. Erasmus had not done nearly enough.

Shammah saw the gaze Erasmus now cast around, at all the women in the city and knew more pain was forthcoming if quick action were not taken. He weighed his options and found himself, and them all, wanting in the balances. He looked helplessly into the face of his closest friend, Hiram, for whom his son had been named. They were both lacking in the ability to stop what was surely coming. What remained of their families could be utterly destroyed now with no chance left for recovery. They had no weapons at hand. And he was no trained soldier.

At most, he could die for his wife. But that would not save her. Maybe if they'd had more time to prepare, they could have made a show of resistance. But not now. Shammah knew the futility, then, of further defiance. They were at the mercy of men who had already proven they had none. Hiram gave a terse nod of agreement. Shammah dropped his head and pointed in the direction he knew the family had taken.

"If you're lying," Erasmus promised, "we WILL be back."

The soldiers passed by them in a blur, in their furor to reach Yosef and his family. Their single crime, presumably, was that they were the only ones thus far to escape the king's wrath. Bereft mothers cradled their babies, now forever sleeping, in their arms while their distraught husbands sought to console them. Inundated with grief, they had no prayers left to spare young Miriam and her son from a similar fate. Maybe it was selfish, but understandably so.

****

Micah

Could this be possible? His heart was filled with dismay at the sight. His eyes were disbelieving. Perhaps he was in a dream, or more accurately, a nightmare. He had no words; his mind groaned in agony. No! Maybe he had somehow happened upon the wrong village. It had been so long since he'd traveled outside its limits. But this? This couldn't be! Mayhem. Destruction. And Blood. Blood everywhere. Even on the very spot where he and Ari had met only a short while ago, there were streaks of red.

The air was saturated with mourning, wailing, moaning, and dying. Smoke rising. Flames shooting! Ruined – the entire village – and Roman soldiers leaving, their mounts nearly trampling

Micah in their haste to depart. He sidestepped them quickly as the small unit bore down on him. But they hardly saw him in any case. He did not matter. He was not the object of their pursuit. The villagers, he saw, had not been as fortunate. They had been unable to avoid the devastation that Erasmus' unit left in its wake. Then a fresh horror was awakened in Micah's mind as he saw the direction the soldiers had taken. It was the very way he had come.

****

The wind had picked up, Ari observed. Even more so as Mal broke down. His disquiet was causing no small disturbance in the atmosphere. Sand and dirt mingled in the air, stirred by the clashing winds. The currents battled each other from different directions, buffeting the escaping party from all sides. Debris rose up and spun around them, creating swirling patterns on the ground. Martha hadn't taken much notice of the changes in the wind's velocity, it seemed to Ari, for she was consumed with the care of Mal. But Ari witnessed how the wind increased in keeping with Mal's turmoil. Ari didn't voice his concern, though, not wanting to cause alarm. He just hoped nothing more came of it.

Yosef looked to his wife, his eyebrows raised in inquiry:

"Perhaps it is time to wake Shuey."

Miriam nodded in response and moved nearer to the toddler, sleeping atop the mule. She shook him gently and murmured to him, their faces close. He turned his face and groaned in protest. He'd only recently fallen asleep. Miriam tried again, this time, blowing softly in his face and talking to him in a sing-song voice:

"Shuey … Shu-ey," she sang to him. Shuey sat up, groggily, rubbing the sleep from his eyes. He reached for her. "Yes, my lamb – come to *Ima*."

Martha, her attention diverted by the exchange, was curious now. The little one hid his face in the curve of his mother's neck. In response to something he said, she uttered:

"Yes. Yes – it *is* time ..."

****

"Ari ..." A familiar voice carried to him over the increasing wind and whirling sands. Ari turned at the sound. His heart quickened a little at the sight of a bedraggled man, coming down the road to meet them. He had on a light colored tunic, similar to what soldiers wore under their armor and sandals (also, reminiscent of their gear) which were strapped high up on his calves in Roman fashion. The man's steps faltered for a moment as he pushed back against a sudden blast of wind. He recovered and picked up his pace, shouting again as if he'd just spotted Ari. The man waved his arm at them as if to draw their attention. Ari's brow puckered in

236

confusion. Who was this coming to meet them? (Not Micah returning, for this man was much taller than Micah.) Clearly, this fellow was not in pursuit but wanted to gain an audience with Ari and his party. But why?

Jules nearly collapsed in relief once he'd sighted Ari and his party, gasping for air. He clutched his chest, for his thudding heart felt ready to explode right out of the cavity. He had been running for a while but surely should not feel this bad. He had severely overtaxed himself. The sounds coming from behind gave him the incentive he needed. Don't fail now, he urged his body. Looking over his shoulder, he gained his feet and covered the remaining distance.

"Ari! Ari!" Jules continued to shout, trying to get out his message, even as he continued to come towards them. He realized that he was still yet too far away for Ari to discern what he said. But he had Ari's attention. The entire party, it seemed, waited on his approach as they were stopped altogether on the road. But he didn't want them waiting. Jules waved them away, trying to convey what words (for he was breathless and out of them) could not. He pantomimed with his arms and hands, but there they stayed still. Were they simple? Could they not understand? He was covered in grime and sweat when he reached Ari, who looked at him in a puzzled way. He grabbed Ari by the shoulders and looked directly into his eyes.

"They're *hah, hah, hah,*" Jules shoulders and chest heaved from the effort expended. He gulped air and tried again. The noises from behind let him know he was out of time. "Run ..." he managed to get out. But Ari still looked as if he didn't understand. He tried to give Ari a little shove. "Go," he got out. Julius' eyes were wild and frantic. "They're –" he broke off as horses thundered around the bend, headed directly towards them.

"They're here," Mal intoned. He spoke in a hollow voice that reverberated as a thousand. But the warning was no longer necessary. Mal's back was to them, and he was on his feet now, they were shocked to find. He stood still as stone, with the full awareness of his foe in the core of his being. Mal turned to meet them full on, his eyes blazing with a holy light from within. His sight was fixed, trance-like, on the regiment in pursuit of him and his friends. The soldiers of his nightmares trampled out of his visions and into actuality. He knew what they'd done to the children. And now they were after this child, too. Rather than induce fear, though, it only strengthened his resolve. He was tired of running. Mal clenched his fists in anticipation. Here was something he could do, he thought. *At last.*

Chapter Twenty-Three

On they came, rider and horse, galloping as one, careening towards their prey. The Strange Man rode with them, nay; he rode the very minds of the soldiers as they drove their horses, directing them. *The child,* a voice said. At first glance, Erasmus didn't see him for the babe was tucked into the shoulder of a woman, likely his mother. Erasmus caught sight of the child when the little boy lifted his head from the folds of her garment. As was the entire party, the child was looking in the direction of the soldiers. His hair lifted in the winds, tufts of locks stirred about his small head. The voice was correct; one child had escaped him! Erasmus pointed at the child and gave a blood-curdling cry, spurring his company forward.

****

"Wha?" Ari couldn't finish the word. His gaze swung back and forth, divided between the unit of soldiers descending furiously upon them and Mal, whose face had taken on a holy zeal.

Martha sat back on her heels, equally torn and alarmed. What was happening? To them and Mal? She knew they had dominion over fire, cloud, water and wind, but what they were experiencing now was something altogether different. They'd only just realized that Ari could heal, and now it appeared Mal was about to do damage of epic proportions. Martha looked at the soldiers incredulously. And all of this was for a child? Mal's countenance was angry, and his voice thundered when he spoke:

"Monsters!" He pointed towards the soldiers as they came. Mal could see now, that they were from his visions. He saw their faces as they committed horrible atrocities towards God's little ones. Memories assaulted him; they washed over him, wave after wave until he was spent. He couldn't even think to formulate complete, coherent thoughts. The children. Their cries and those of their mothers came to him, once again. Too late, Mal realized that he'd failed to preserve those children in an effort to save the one. Merely the thought, the guilt alone, drove him to the point of madness. He wanted the blood of those responsible. Murderers, he thought grimly. Retribution was coming. He would make them pay.

"To me," Mal cried out to his companions. Stretching his arms out on both sides, he pulled the winds to him as he prepared to defend his friends. "Hold on to me!" Ari didn't wait to be told twice. From the angrily twirling winds that seemed to be in synchronization with Mal's mood, he knew something was about to happen, and it couldn't be good. He grabbed Jules' arm and pulled him down to Martha's side. Yosef, with Miriam and the child, were on Mal's opposite side. Yosef shielded them both with his body, his robe whipping about with the rising wind.

"Vengeance is mine, says the Lord," Mal yelled, eyes ablaze, speaking with the voice of a multitude. Indeed, he looked like an avenging angel of legend. It was a pronouncement of judgment against the soldiers. A blast of wind shot out from him, creating a circumference of air about them which formed a wall of protection for Mal and his friends. With his outstretched arms, Mal made a wide circling motion over his head, and the wind obeyed.

Ari and Martha watched as the wind mimicked the direction of Mal's hand. As his hand gained more speed, so went the wind. The midmorning sky became as dark as Mal's wrath. The current increased in ferocity until the detritus became so thick as to be nearly impassable. Still, the soldiers came, driven by the one to whom they had yielded their members to obey. They were servants of the Strange Man now, instruments and tools to be used in his service. Onward, onward they came, and the recognizable golden-green light flared in the soldiers' eyes. Mal, Ari, and Martha knew it all too well. This was no mere cavalry. They were led and imbued with supernatural ability from the Strange Man.

"You dare come for *this* child?" A disembodied voice thundered, so loud now that it came from without Mal. Even at the frightful sound, the men were not discouraged. They didn't check their speed but urged their steeds forward, intent on flinging themselves at the barrier of winds. The turbulent force increased even more so, becoming funnel-like. The tail end of the tornado snaked out and caught the lead soldier. Erasmus was snatched up by the destructive torrent before he had time to scream. Horse and rider were caught up in a whirlwind, legs flailing ineffectively, looking for purchase of the ground. Alópéx, ever at Erasmus' side, in life and deed, was next.

Yank! Yank! Yank! It was purposeful. The wind became sentient, bent to Mal's will and able to deliberately target and pluck up the soldiers. The wind operated in conjunction with Mal, becoming an extension of him, reaching out like his hand. One by one, the storm caught them all until only one soldier remained. At the last moment, he tried to turn away. But it was too late – there would be no escape for him. The last soldier was quickly gathered and tossed into the melee. He joined the others to form a macabre dance of riders and horses, spinning around above Mal's head.

As they watched, the legs of the horses stopped churning, and the golden-green light died out of the eyes of the soldiers. It was over. Or should have been. But Mal was up on his feet now, swinging his arm wildly now, and the gale responded, becoming choppy and unfocused. Mal wasn't losing control of the wind, for it obeyed his every whim. He was, however, losing control of himself while in the throes of his gift.

The storm began to transform right before their eyes. While Mal wreaked havoc on the enemy, his friends had remained safe in the center of the turmoil. Now there was a shift, and the circle began to close in upon them. Though his implements of destruction were ruined, the Strange Man, it seemed, was far from done.

"You dare come for this child?" Mal shouted into the wind again. "I will kill you all!" He would make them pay. *Destroy*, Mal thought, destroy them all. Ari knew from the golden sheen now rolling over Mal's eyes that they were all in trouble.

****

"You will pay! Vengeance is MINE!" Ari heard Mal scream at the soldiers, who were now beyond knowledge of their evil deeds and this world. Caught in the court of Mal's justice, he had shown no mercy. But they had already received their just compensation. Ari wasn't worried about them, as he watched the eye of Mal's storm slowly shrinking. Kill them all, was about right. Mal was about to bring destruction upon the very heads of the friends he'd worked so hard to protect if he wasn't stopped. Ari jumped up and grabbed Mal's shoulders and gave him a shake, trying to bring Mal out of his furor.

"Mal," Ari tried to get through to his friend. "Mal! You'll kill us all," and Ari shook Mal again. But Mal threw Ari aside. He would not be deterred. Mal and the wind were an unstoppable force.

So much misery, Mal had seen. So much destruction by the soldiers. In this world, so much sorrow. He couldn't take it. Why not? Why not just end it all? Despair overtook him. He felt helpless against its pull. We should all die, he thought, as he saw the horses and riders churning and colliding in the darkened sky. Argh! His heart cried at the ghastly sight, bursting at its seams. He had brought them to their end.

I am like them, he thought. Now, I am a murderer, too. And that thought pierced his heart like a knife. His face was drenched with tears as his personal storm raged. Help me, Lord! The condemnation rested heavily on his chest. What did it matter anymore? Let the wind take me, he thought as the storm came closer. Let it take us. Lord, help us all.

Just then, the little one lifted his head from his mother's bosom as if his name had been called. Yosef was a heavy weight, pinning Shuey and his mother to Mal's side. Shuey moved the cloth aside that was covering his head and looked up. The skies brewed, filled with objects he didn't fully comprehend, but he knew something was wrong. He took in the distress of his new friend, Mal, and the fear of those who had embarked upon this journey with his family. Shuey saw the tempest drawing nigh to them all.

Martha held fast to Mal's legs. She had wrapped her body and limbs around him as much as possible and was holding on for all she was able. The wind tugged at her small frame and threatened to carry her away.

"Mal! What are you doing?" She screamed up at him in terror, but her voice was lost in the loud drone of the windstorm. Still, she had to try. She struck his leg with her fist, only releasing her grasp as much as she dared. "Mal, you MUST STOP!" But his storm raged on, oblivious to the appeals of his cousin.

Ari had left the comparative safety and shelter of Mal's body when he'd gotten up in an attempt to bring Mal to his senses. Now, the wind sucked greedily at Ari, seeking to draw him into its destructive power. Acting quickly, Julius reached out and pulled Ari to him, but it wasn't enough. Jules then threw himself across Ari's slighter body and pressed down to the ground, hoping he could anchor them. The wind tore at them both, but Jules held on.

Shuey's eyes grew big at that. The sight of Ari, very nearly being swept away, was enough to alarm him. Somehow, he knew Mal was responsible for this storm. He didn't want Mal to hurt Ari or any of them. Just as Jules and Ari began to lose their battle against the wind, lifting them into the air, the little boy cried out.

The wail of the child reached Mal, whereas the entreaties of his friends could not. At the child's utterance, Mal's personal storm ceased to wage. He collapsed on the ground, falling on his knees; the winds and all they contained fell with him. Mal looked at his hands in disbelief and sobbed. He held his face and cried at the realization of what he'd done in his killing rage and what he'd almost done to his friends. He had given in to despair and nearly brought an end to them all.

And for what? Because he could not bear to see the evil. When measuring strength, to date, he'd always thought of the physical. He had been infatuated with the idea of being as strong as his father one day. He'd liked the idea that the wind could make him even more so. Now the reality of that terrified him. He'd never thought of the mental aspect, the fortitude to endure pain and hardship. His mom had that kind of strength. It could see you through the bad until you could live to see the good again. And there was still good in this world. Of this, the toddler was proof. That the little boy was alive was also evidence that Mal, himself, could be responsible for good.

Then Shuey, as he was near Mal's shoulder, climbed out of his mother's arms and pulled himself up and onto Mal. Judging things to be safe now, Miriam let Shuey go to Mal haltingly. In light of what Mal had just done, she didn't know just what to think. He'd saved them, yes. But, he was also in possession of a terrible power. Shuey seemed to think Mal was safe enough, though. He leaned over and peered into Mal's face until the bigger boy met his eyes. Miriam saw there was no fear of Mal in Shuey's face.

In spite of what he'd just done, Mal felt the unconditional love that only a child could give. And, inexplicably, forgiveness. Shuey was not afraid of him and still saw Mal as his friend. *A friend that almost destroyed them all,* Mal thought, berating himself again. Mal could not be as forgiving of himself as little Shuey. But then, a tiny hand touched Mal's face, questing and smoothing away the frown lines. As Shuey wiped away Mal's tears, peace came over Mal such as he had never known.

When he looked to his friends again, Mal's eyes were normal, brown and red-rimmed from crying. But very normal, Mal eyes.

"Oh, Mal!" Martha dropped to his side. Miriam extricated a squirming Shuey and let Martha take over. Shame engulfed Mal, and Martha held him as he cried again. Between sobs, he looked around at the remains of their enemies, lying about on the ground. They were testimony to his vengeance, unleashed. Mal recalled that he had wanted to dash them against the rocks in his fury. But he saw that was no longer necessary. As with himself, they no longer held that garish light in their eyes. The Strange Man was gone, defeated for the time being.

Mal's eyes welled with fresh tears again, at the damage he had wrought. Was any of this needful? Yes, he answered himself. The soldiers came for the life of Shuey. It was necessary to protect the child. He would have done it many times over to protect them, all of those babies, had he been able. Even though justified and knowing the evil they had done, he did not enjoy seeing the mangled bodies of his enemies. It broke something in him. His shoulders quaked as he wept.

A cry escaped, again, from the lad. He stirred in his mother's arms, wanting to be put down. She obliged when she saw him reaching towards Mal, arms outstretched. Mal picked him up gladly. The hug the little one gave him restored his faith in himself and humanity. For the little one's sake, he quashed his tears and sobered his expression. The visions that had plagued him since the start of their journey were silenced, at last. And his headache, that horrible throbbing, was gone. Never to return, he hoped. But he would always have memories of the atrocities he'd witnessed.

Chapter Twenty-Four

The air around them was filled with residual grit, settling as the winds died in tandem with Mal's level of grief over the lost lives and the part he'd played in their demise. Mal had been inconsolable over his act until he held the child. Martha saw that even her ministrations held no sway over his pain. She was unable to assuage his guilt and horror over his actions. But the child – under his touch, the hurricane of Mal's emotions gradually calmed. The winds decreased to a gentle breeze and then came to rest altogether. The granules of mingled dirt and sand covered everything, which was a good thing. Some things weren't meant to be seen. But the suggestion, the clues of what had happened, remained. A lump here, the imprint of a leg there, hooves sticking out unnaturally, was all that remained of the soldiers that had come for them. Mal tried to shield the young boy from the carnage, but it was all around them. Still, he tried. No need for them both to have nightmares about this day.

Martha averted her eyes from the gruesome sight as much as she was able. Ari took it all in with a shudder and thought to himself: This is what Mal's gift, unchecked, can do? This was the power he wielded? No longer benign in Ari's eyes, he saw the gifts for their capacity for damage. The words of the Young Master came back to him, full of meaning:

"All I ask is that you use your gifts *responsibly.*"

At the time, the extra emphasis on that one word, *responsibly*, didn't register. But it did now. The weight of that duty fell on him as he surveyed the destruction all around and saw Mal's miserable state over what he had done. Now Ari understood.

This is what happened when they allowed themselves to be vengeful when displaying their talents. Their gifts could be used for *other* than good.

Mal had just snapped under so great a pressure. Ari couldn't help but wonder if he and Martha would be subject to the same trial. Would they also break? Watching the two of them, Mal and Shuey, Ari felt it must have been worth it all. It had to be. For there the child sat, unharmed, in Mal's arms. Ari couldn't fathom who this child would become or why he was so important. Mal's actions declared that the little one was worth protecting. As the breeze gentled and brought into clear focus the chaos all around him, Ari had a grim thought: he didn't ever want to get Mal riled up.

"Come, Shuey," Miriam said to her son as she disentangled him, once again, from Mal's embrace. Her husband nodded his head in agreement as if he knew her thoughts.

"Yes, we must be on our way," Yosef agreed. "There may be others."

"But where?" Jules broke in abruptly and then recoiled at the boldness of his question. He had been huddled on the ground with the rest of them, helpless under the onslaught of Mal's destructive power. Now Jules cowered once more, as the force of their gaze rested on him. *Surely, I must be in the presence of heavenly beings,* he thought, and paid them proper obeisance, on his knees before them.

"Where will you go?" Jules asked of them, again. His voice trembled some, and he bowed low to the ground, humbled before them. *Please don't hurt me,* he pled silently, hoping he did not offend them with his inquisitiveness. He didn't understand much about what just happened but considered what he had witnessed. He had so many questions he wanted to put to them. What manner of people had he stumbled upon, Ari and his friends, that could cause the anger of King Herod to descend upon them? And who was Mal that he commanded the wind, and it obeyed his whim? And what child was this that he would garner such powerful guardians? All these questions, Jules pondered. But the next one that broke forth from his lips was:

"Can I come?"

****

Jules spoke before he could stop himself as if compelled. *Take me with you*, his heart cried. A hardened Roman soldier, he had witnessed much. But never this. Suddenly, he only wanted to be in their company. He wasn't even sure what he yearned for more – to learn more about Ari and their connection, to witness more displays of supernatural power, or to follow the destiny of the precious child to see what he would become. All were equally intriguing. Until now his ambition had been to receive a promotion and to rise in the ranks of the legion. But at that moment, Jules didn't want to be a soldier anymore. He wanted to drop everything, give it all up and follow them, follow

Ari. He wanted, he needed, to get to know him. Jules felt, now more than ever, a connection between himself and this young man.

"Take me with you," he said, this time audibly.

Ari considered his father's words as he took Jules by the elbow and raised him to his feet. Mal and Martha looked to Ari for answers and wouldn't meet Jules' eyes. It wasn't for them to deny or consent to Jules' request. He didn't know what he was asking. They weren't even sure that they could grant his wish. They wondered, separately, if Ari could see as they saw. Could Ari even make the right decision regarding his beloved father whom he missed so much? But to answer Jules was up to Ari. An uncomfortable expression clouded Ari's face as he cleared his throat and gathered his thoughts.

"Pa-" *Pater*, he'd almost said, catching himself in time. "Jules, I – we would love to have you with us," he gestured to include Mal and Martha. They nodded in agreement. "But you can't come," he sighed, looking morose at the thought. Ari recalled the many times his father had said these same words as he left their home to begin his day as commanding officer of his battalion. Ari would look at his father, beseeching with his gaze, only to be given the negative reply. It was strange to have their roles reversed; the words broke Ari's heart to utter. Jules didn't even know Ari was his son, yet he risked his career (as well as, life and limb) in coming here to warn a stranger who bore his features. Jules may not have known Ari consciously, but perhaps his heart recognized that Ari was his son.

Jules frowned at Ari's declaration and looked puzzled. Why could he not go? But Ari knew his father had to go back. His mom was bereft without her husband now. What would become of her if she'd never met him? For that matter, what would become of Ari? No, he shook his head as he summed up his decision. His father could not come. He was needed here. His internal debate was put to an end, just as Jules opened his mouth to further plead his cause. Ari stepped closer to his father. Jules looked at Ari expectantly, his expression hopeful. The determined set of Ari's features registered a moment before Jules' vision clouded over and was gone.

Chapter Twenty-Five

Jules stretched his hands out before him, seeking Ari but only touching air, for Ari had stepped back once more. Martha and Mal, though they had witnessed the whole thing, were at a loss to explain what had just happened. They saw Ari wave his hand as he stepped before Jules, who now stared out at them from sightless eyes. His irises, normally just a tad bluer than Ari's, swirled cloudy and gray.

"Wha - what have you done to me?" Jules gasped. Water welled and then waved across his irises obscuring his vision. He blinked his eyes and rubbed them, trying to clear his sight.

"Only what I must," Ari replied without inflection. As he swallowed, a lump formed and swelled, threatening to close his throat. He felt empty inside at the action he'd just taken. To leave his father here was to sentence him to certain death, eventually; this much Ari knew. He had seen his father's demise. To stay here with Jules or to go back with his friends, to his mom and life seemed to be his only options. But did he have another? Could he take Jules back with him? He turned it over in his mind. To take Julius could mean no meeting with Mom and thus, no Ari. Also, what would happen to Jules if he suddenly reappeared in a world that thought him already dead? And older? Jules could not just resume his life where he had left off. The implications dizzied him until he recalled the words of the YM.

"I need you to live your life," he'd said to Ari, "the life you are destined to live, *here* and *now*."

At the time, all Ari could think of was seeing his father again. The words tormented Ari now, for he felt the truth of them sinking into the marrow of his bones. Jules *had* to stay and live the life he was meant to live. As he thought more on the words of the young prophet, Ari felt more certain that this was the thing to do. Besides, the blinding effect had to be temporary. It had to do with his will, right? His gift was influenced by intention. He argued with himself. It had to be well. After all, it wasn't like Ari could order his dad to stay behind.

"But ... why?" Jules couldn't understand what he could have done to warrant such treatment.

"You need to go back, Father," Ari said in a rush, and then could have kicked himself. He tried to cover his slip with more speech. "You cannot follow," came Ari's sad reply. Jules puckered his brow in confusion. More than the note of true regret in Ari's voice, Jules zeroed in on one last word. Wait - *Father*?

"Ari, how - I don't understand ..." But Ari would say no more. He had already spoken too much. Jules continued to call for him, reaching for him. He took a few steps forward, gingerly.

A soft neigh nearby broke his concentration. Jules turned his head at the sounds. Stomping hooves. The snorting of a horse. He strained his ears, listening for more. Had they left him already? What was happening? He craned his head at every sound.

To his friends, Ari pursed his lips and motioned for them to keep silent. Let Julius think they were gone. After all the destruction, there was a lone horse miraculously alive. The brown stallion rose from the sand, snorting and stamping his hooves as he tested the firm ground underneath. Julius' head whipped around at the sounds, his eyes trained in that direction, although he still could not see. Ari went to the horse slowly, contrition in his every step. He grasped the reins and led him to Julius.

Jules reached out as the horse came near to him. Patting about the muscular flanks of the animal, he located and grasped the reins. Years of training had him swinging up into the saddle, sight unseen. He could do that in his sleep. But what did it all mean? Were they, he and the horse, all that

266

remained as witnesses to this terrible event? Jules' sighed wistfully, knowing that he was privy to a divinely ordained encounter. How he wished he could have continued with them and ... his *son*. Shaking his head at the incredulity of it all, Jules gathered the reins to himself and softly said to the animal:

"Let's go home."

****

Ari watched silently as the well-trained war horse headed back towards Jerusalem. He aided the beast with a little tug of the harness and push in the right direction. His eyes watered as his dear father departed from his life once more. He could only hope that, during his travels, they would have occasion to cross paths again. Until then, he would be thankful for this opportunity to have seen his beloved *patér*, again. Jules was youthful and alive and full of vitality, just the way Ari would want to remember his father. Ari would hold onto this memory and treasure it, always. He wiped at dry eyes. They stung. He would not cry. He would not. His throat constricted from the effort. He had shed tears aplenty from the last separation. He just hoped he'd see Jules again. One day. The more he thought on it, the surer he became.

"I'll see you again, Father," Ari vowed quietly.

Chapter Twenty-Six

Martha and Mal joined Ari and heard his affirmation. Yes, they supposed, Ari would see his father again for he had not even been born yet. That was the whole point of sending Jules back. He had a destiny yet to fulfill.

As Mal watched Jules leave, he felt ... normal. No voices in his head. No screams. No visions blinding him in their ferocity; none of that remained. Just ... peace. The first respite he'd had in what seemed like a long, long time. Except for his own thoughts, his head was quite empty. He smiled to himself ironically, and he thought of the fun Ari could have with that. Ari, who was now in pain over the loss, once again, of his father. Mal nudged his friend with his shoulder just to let him know he was there. Martha, ever the mother hen, put her hand in Ari's to let him know that she, too, was there for him. Not much either of them could say, but they said it nearly simultaneously:

"Bye, Jules."

"Mal!" After leaving the grisly scene behind them, the group had traveled just up the road a piece when the toddler created a minor disruption. He fretted something terrible, in an attempt to get out of his mother's arms. But she held him fast as she tried to get him on the mule. He squirmed indignantly and reached in the direction of the children. As Mal covered the short distance between them, he could see the eyes of the child tracking him. Shuey wanted Mal, and he let them all know with a loud protest. Shuey reached for Mal as Mal did the same.

"Hush, little one," he spoke to the child in soothing tones, as he would to his younger sister, Hannah. "Why all the fuss?" The toddler held Mal's face between cherubic hands and gazed into his eyes. He patted Mal's cheeks gently, exploring the crevices of his face, pinching at intervals with tiny fingers. He looked at Mal as if he wanted to capture that face, those features, to store forever in his memory. Mal understood. He wouldn't forget his little friend either. Their connection just *was*. Mal didn't bother trying to define it.

"Mal go bye?" Shuey said as he looked intently into Mal's eyes. Mal looked to Miriam for an explanation.

"I told him it was time we were on our way and that we had to bid farewell to our new friends," she admitted, a trifle sheepishly. "It's what got him all riled."

Ari and Martha stepped forward to console the child, but he was already smiling at Mal. He clapped his hands together gleefully and hugged Mal, nearly rocking Mal back in his enthusiasm. He'd only wanted to say goodbye. Shuey pulled back and looked at Ari and Martha.

"Martha go bye, too?" She nodded her head in reply. Sitting in Mal's arms, he was above her head.

"Yes, Shuey." She reached for his chubby hand, gave it a kiss and held his palm to her face. Her eyes misted. He really was a sweet child. Shuey turned to Ari.

"Ari go bye?" Shuey asked again. This time, his voice and expression were incredulous as if he couldn't believe all of his new friends would be taken at once. Ari nodded with a small smile for Shuey.

"Yes, little man." Ari patted the toddler on his back. *My little man* was how his father often referred to him. Ari figured it was time to pass that nickname on. "Time for us to go." And he supposed it was true. They had gotten the child to relative safety and sent Julius on his way. What more reason was there to stay?

"Yes, Shuey – all of them go bye, and so must we." Miriam went to each of them and gave a little squeeze of their shoulders in passing. She hesitated a second before touching Mal. She didn't know if she should. Though he had the look of a young boy, he displayed the power of a heavenly being. When he looked at her in expectation, she reached around his broad shoulders and gave him a squeeze, too. He looked grateful. Mal didn't want her to be afraid of him. He was already frightened of himself.

Miriam realized that Mal was just like any other child and needed affection. His reaction to her touch indicated that he knew a mother's love, but where was his own? Her heart went out to him, to them all. Though not significantly older than them, they appealed to her maternal instinct. Miriam was moved to press upon them to stay so that she could care for them. Yosef obviously felt the same for he came to stand at her side and offered:

"Would you journey with us further?"

But Mal smiled and shook his head. He was thankful for their concern, but their time with the young couple and their son was over. He felt it. He knew it. The purpose for which Mal and his friends were sent had been accomplished.

Yosef and Miriam didn't push further and resigned themselves to the wishes of the children. The husband spoke a benediction over their traveling companions while Miriam said a silent prayer for the children who had become their protectors. She prayed that The One True God would bless and keep them until they were in the arms of their loved ones again. Shuey, no longer distraught, had begun to bounce in Mal's arms. He recognized the departure blessing that his father pronounced, having heard it on many occasions and took this as a signal to leave. He made a game of it, singing:

"Mal go bye, Martha go bye, Ari go bye!" As Shuey sang each name, he would lean forward and touch the appropriate head or face as best as his diminutive arms would allow. The children let out a cheer at the end of Shuey's song because they knew it made him happy. There was something about him, Martha thought. He was somehow ... familiar. Martha had a glimpse of playing on the beach and huddling around ... but before she could grasp hold of the thought, it was gone. The baby clapped his hands together joyfully and went in for another round:

"Mal go bye, Martha go bye, Ari go bye!" Shuey grinned at them and waved. "Go BYE-BYE!" He dropped to the ground suddenly, landing on his little feet. He looked about him and ran to Miriam, finger in mouth. His eyes were wide, and his expression filled with surprise. Her expression matched his, with more besides, for Mal, Martha, and Ari were gone.

"Shu-ey?" Miriam elongated his name, not knowing what had happened to the children but feeling sure they would be fine. Shuey smiled shyly at his mother. Yosef shook his head.

"Let us be on our way."

Chapter Twenty-Seven

The children found themselves, quite abruptly, at the beach. They immediately pointed fingers and narrowed suspicious eyes. Their expressions mirrored shock and puzzlement as they asked in unison:

"Which one of you did that?"

"Me? You!" Came the response. But it was an impossible conclusion, surely? Didn't they *all* have to be in agreement to make translation possible? Not one person of their troika could do that by their will alone.

A realization came to Martha, and she held up her hand as a fleeting thought occurred to her, took form and suddenly became corporeal. The wondrous expression on her face left the boys anticipating. Mal looked at her expectantly. Ari made a gesture with his hands to indicate she should continue. Yes! She nodded her head in confirmation.

That had to be it; she concluded and answered with finality.

"Shuey did it."

What? How was that even possible? Ari and Mal erupted at once, ridiculing her theory before she even got the chance to expound.

"A *child* doesn't have that kind of power," Mal denied hotly. It didn't make sense.

"We do," she countered.

"Also, how would he know where to send us?" Disbelief was evident in Ari's voice, his tone equal to a verbal pat on her head. Ugh! That made Martha so mad! They hadn't even heard her out. But before she could respond, another voice interjected.

"Martha is correct," the Young Master said calmly.

Relief flooded her face, and she turned to hurl herself into his arms.

****

Mal and Ari looked on with happy surprise as the Young Master caught Martha and took her up, swinging her about as if she were no larger than Shuey. Martha captured his face in her hands and gazed adoringly into his eyes. She suddenly grinned so hard, a face splitting smile that only his presence seemed to bring out.

"You figured it out." He smiled back at her and nodded approvingly.

"Well, yes–" she began, but Ari broke in.

"Wait – figured out what?" He was truly at a loss as to what was going on.

"I knew from your eyes," Martha continued as if Ari hadn't spoken. She appeared mesmerized, all of her attention taken up as her own eyes feasted on his features. "They haven't changed."

Ari was still puzzled. His puckered brow revealed his consternation.

"Should I tell them?" Martha asked of the Young Master. She wasn't feeling especially generous towards Ari at the moment, especially considering his earlier treatment of her. She hated being patronized. Because of her size, she had rather a chip on her shoulder about it.

"Martha," the Young Master gently admonished.

She grinned again, her good mood restored and quickly gave in. She hadn't the heart to keep it from them any longer, even though they didn't deserve it.

"Ari, Mal," she announced triumphantly, "meet Shuey."

****

The looks on their faces as their jaws dropped were comical, thought Martha smugly. Almost worth what they'd put her through. She could nearly visualize them mentally scratching their heads. She wanted to laugh out loud – but that would be mean. She didn't want to be mean. She wanted to be right.

"My mother always says the eyes never change." Her mom maintained that she would know her children, simply by their eyes. She claimed that Martha's eyes, especially, had not altered in appearance from the day she was born and held for the first time. When Martha saw Shuey, there had been something familiar about him. His eyes reminded her of someone she loved, whose face she'd studied for subtle nuances, answers, and clues.

"When the thought first occurred to me, I admit, I thought I was just being fanciful," she owned ruefully. "But I couldn't help but see you."

She smiled shyly at the Young Master. It was in the child's eyes, now become so familiar to her, as well as his mannerisms.

"Of course!" Ari thumped his fist in his hand, for emphasis. It was if a veil had been lifted. "Why didn't I see it then?" His mind flashed back and recalled the miracle, the healing of the beggar's deformed hand. He'd felt power course through him, as well as Shuey, enveloping them both and flowing into the man as he was made whole. He mentally kicked himself, for he recognized that power. It was evident from their first encounter with the YM. He should have known.

"Martha had ... a little help," the Young Master added.

"But I didn't know for certain until he sent us back," Martha admitted. She did know that Shuey conjured some of the same feelings in her as the Young Master, and felt loved beyond belief, in ways that were unfathomable. At the time, Martha credited that to the simple love of a child. But there was more, even then, coming from Shuey. That love emanated from the Young Master and evoked a similar reaction within her – feelings that were a mere reflection of what he felt for her. He claimed her utter devotion.

Throughout this whole exchange, Mal stood silently by and watched. He got it. He understood now that it was the young prophet all along. It made sense that only His touch could calm Mal, soothe the spells of madness, and provide a balm for his torturous visions. But Mal was suddenly angry. Justifiably so, he felt. The Young Master looked in Mal's direction as if he knew what Mal was thinking.

"Mal–" the young prophet began but was cut off.

"Why?" Ari and Martha turned at Mal's tortured whisper. "You did this?" he said again to the Young Master, demanding answers. "Why would you do this to me?" His voice wobbled as Mal recalled the visions and horrors he'd beheld. Tears spilled over and down his cheeks as he railed. He felt older for the experience as if he would never forget, never be young again. He knew things now, had witnessed things that no one, let alone a child, should ever have to see. He was appalled by all he'd seen and the things he could do. Through his tears, he saw the young prophet beckoning to him. But his feet stayed rooted to the spot. He was mired in misery, overcome with grief. He shook his head sorrowfully at the Young Master, wanting no part of this "gift" any longer.

The words of the young prophet came to him, spoken to him at the onset, upon the bestowing of his talent:

"Malachi – you are named after a great prophet ... and so you shall be."

Strong arms encircled him, girding him up. The face of the Young Master swam before him; concern showing upon his features. The young prophet had come to Mal. He had come *for* Mal, closing the distance between them so certainly that Mal felt it would always be so. The YM would not give up on Mal easily. Mal saw then that his own pain was also the prophet's pain. He knew everything that Mal went through, saw each horrendous vision Mal had viewed. He also knew what Mal had done – Mal saw it in the prophet's eyes. But forgiveness was also in the YM's gaze.

And, oh! The same love he'd felt from Shuey was held therein. It overwhelmed Mal. And that peace, again. It comforted and soothed Mal's troubled spirit as if calming a turbulent storm. He'd felt that same stillness come over him when Shuey had touched him. If he had any lingering doubts about Martha's assertion, they were laid to rest. He gave the young prophet a weak smile, ashamed of his outburst now.

"Because you are His messenger, the things that break the heart of God will break your heart also. I understand and feel your pain," the Young Master said to Mal. And Mal could feel that was true. Grief and contrition rose up in Mal like bile in his throat when he recalled his acts, once again. There was no forgiveness in his heart for himself. His eyes brimmed with tears until they, indeed, spilled over.

"There will come a time of reckoning, of recompense," the Young Master promised darkly. "But it is not for us to decide."

Mal nodded and recalled the righteous rage he felt over the innocent lives that were lost. He quickly squelched those feelings because they overwhelmed him. His own abilities terrified him.

"What happened -" he began, but Mal knew what had happened. He ducked his head guiltily, avoiding the eyes of the Young Master. He would know all. Surely he would know. So Mal confessed, "I lost control of my gift." He hung his head in shame.

"Not lost. You gave your control away to another," the Young Master responded. "When you determined to use your gift to get vengeance and justice for *yourself*, you became susceptible to being used, you and your gift, for a purpose other than intended."

"Great care," the Young Master continued, "must be exercised with the use of your talent." Mal hung his head and remembered. He'd felt so out of control but, at the same time that he was being controlled. He must master his gift. The stakes were too high if he did not. His mind supplied the *or else*: he would risk bringing harm to himself and others.

Worse yet, he could expose his gift to being used for great evil.

"Ari!" A thought suddenly occurred to Martha, "Whatever happened to Jules?" Was he blind, still? Did he yet live? Perhaps they had done something to change the past, she thought hopefully.

"He is – was fine. Jules recovered his sight after he got back to the barracks," Ari replied, somberly. New memories came to him then, supplanting the old. He knew and could feel they had changed. "I remember him telling me the story of how he had been part of a battle where he'd barely escaped with his life." Ari touched his face as he mused and smiled grimly at the thought. "He was rewarded for bravery in battle. That commendation eventually led to his becoming a centurion."

"Is he ...?" Martha's face lit up at the thought.

"No," Ari shook his head in response. That memory had not changed, maybe the circumstances, but his father remained gone. Ari's face was grave and resigned. He had to accept that, once and for all. Maybe his father was destined for demise no matter what circumstances altered in his timeline. There was one more thing he wanted to say to the Young Master, though. As he stepped forward, Martha cringed, waiting for Ari to hurl accusations at the Young Master in the same fashion as Mal.

"Thank you," Ari simply said, "for letting me see my father again." His eyes glimmered with unshed tears for a moment before Ari willed them back. "It meant the world to me." He fell on the Young Master for a moment, allowing his hair to be caressed for a short time before he pulled away. Ari straightened and wiped his face with the backside of his hand.

He was not crying, Ari told himself, and should not be sad. He had been given a second chance, an opportunity not afforded to any, he'd wager. Saying farewell the second time was harder, though. Ari blinked, and he forced back tears, once more. He would be grateful, he ordered himself, sternly. Ari nodded his head tersely at the Young Master to let him know he understood what had been done for him. It was a reprieve from his grief over the loss of his father. It changed nothing.

But it did bring to mind yet another question from Martha. What of the beggar they'd come across? And how was it that Ari was able to heal him? Did they all have that capability? Was the healing reversed after they'd left, as in the case of Jules temporary blindness? So many questions, she had. She spun around, determined to get answers from the prophet, but the first in a barrage of queries hung in the air, incomplete:

"Whatever happened to ...?" But he was no longer there.

"That is for you to discover," the voice of the Young Master came to them, trailing off and echoing, they now realized, into an early morning sky. Was it the same morning they'd left? Too many questions, not enough answers, Martha grumbled to herself. Before frustration set in over the lack thereof, they heard the sounds of someone coming towards them. A gentle tinkling sound announced his approach.

He was a little fellow; that much could be seen in the increasing sunlight. Martha shielded her eyes from the glowing orb, now half of a fiery ball on the horizon before them, trying to see who was coming to meet them. His gait seeming vaguely familiar, but she couldn't place it. She tried to make out his features as he shortened the distance between them. Who would be headed to the beach so early and for what purpose? Go see, a voice prodded.

He was weighed down with a cumbersome bundle he carried across his shoulders. The little goat that he led trotted obediently beside the man, carrying a similar package. As he drew near to the group of children, memories flooded them. Recognition dawned on their faces. The man, childlike in height, looked up and greeted them with a big grin.

"Well! I didn't expect to have patrons so early in the morning, especially as I've not had the chance to set up shop, yet!" He gave them a keen look and lowered his burden to the ground. The children exchanged puzzled glances as the little man unrolled his package, displaying his wares. Martha gasped. Toys! The make of which she'd never seen.

"But we have no coin," Ari began.

"And I'll have none of that," the fellow rejoined, quite in a jovial mood. "I give," he insisted, "as I am led." He talked and hummed to himself the entire time as he rummaged through his wares, waving off their protestations. Mumbling things like, "just the thing ... yes ... ah!" before Martha found in her hands, a daintily carved house, perfect for child's play. Mal received a beautifully formed dancing girl – for which he inclined his head in gratitude. He would give it to Hannah. The last object was held up to the sunlight for final inspection before being placed into Ari's hands. Micah, for it was he, folded his hands firmly over Ari's as he did it.

"You have the look of someone I once met, long ago," the older man's eyes misted over as he spoke. This version of Micah had lines that creased his face, as well as, graying hair. But the joy he'd displayed when he'd first been healed was still apparent. "One who performed a service for me that I could never repay, but I should like to." He patted Ari's hand and smiled warmly. "But you cannot be he," Micah asserted, but his eyes searched Ari's face as if he were still considering. The little man finally shook his head.

"Thank you!" The response left Ari in a gush of genuine gratitude. He held in his hands the flute his father had given him, the same as he left with little Shuey. Wonder and awe lit his features. Instead of being made of freshly carved wood like the others, the flute was worn and burnished from use. Ari supposed it truly must have been a good gift for a little boy; fit for a king.

"It was given to me by a man one day, who simply asked that I would put it in the hands of one who could appreciate it." Micah turned to take his leave of them. He moved to gather his creations, which had spilled out of his bag, in his search for the perfect item to give. The children helped him to pack up his things and mount them on his shoulders, once more.

"Come Jezebel!" The goat obediently followed, the bell on her neck tinkling delicately as she went.

"Bye Micah!" the trio called to him, waving as he left. Of course, they knew his name. And Micah would not think it strange. Their newly implanted memories supplied the information: Micah was now an inventor of, among other things, toys. On certain days, he liked to come down to the beach, or the marketplace and entertain children. But his special joy seemed to be in pairing just the right toy with the right child. They watched until he was gone from sight.

Looking at Micah's departing figure, Ari was humbled at the thought of being used to help this man in such a way. That is, Ari had allowed himself to become a vessel. He had opened himself to the possibility from the moment he'd reached for the beggar. And he didn't feel equal to this calling, this gift to heal others. But, obviously, that did not matter. The gift was his, just the same.

"Well," Mal suddenly announced into the silence, bone weary and mentally exhausted. "Let's go home."

Chapter Twenty-Eight

Mal

... walked in the door with kindling under his arm, which he deposited in the diminished pile for later use. *Ima* looked up, gratefully, from where she kneeled baking her flat bread. His sister, Abigail, took over and flipped the bread quickly while Mother greeted Mal. He bent to kiss her cheek.

"Oof!" All the air was suddenly expelled from his stomach in a rush as a tiny figure threw herself at him. Of course, she was a she, he thought, for he was the only male in his father's absence. He was already accounted for and now, so was Hannah.

"Ma-al!" She always said his name with two syllables, especially when she was put out. Which, at the moment, she most definitely was. "Where did you go?" She pouted, "I was supposed to wake you up, but you weren't there!" Her tone indicated that she felt altogether cheated. She gave him a mournful look, normally guaranteed to break him. Not today. Mal felt tired. The weight of his gift, the responsibility, the whole ordeal suddenly sat so heavily on his shoulders. But he always made time for Hannah. She loved her big brother so. Maybe because he indulged her. Too much. Then Mal recalled the gift Micah had given him.

"That's because I have something for you," he said, by way of explanation. Hannah would bite. She always did. So predictable. Her big-eyed, pitiful look turned to one of expectancy. "Close your eyes." He placed the figurine in her outstretched hands.

As soon as Hannah felt the object fall in her palms, her face stretched into the biggest grin imaginable. She opened her eyes, oohing and aahing at the sight of the exquisitely formed dancer.

"Oh, Mal!" Hannah breathed and despite his utter bone weariness, he felt his face responding. This last foray into the past revealed just how much power he wielded. But it also taught him the importance of doing so responsibly. However, in this one area (pleasing Hannah, that is), he excelled.

"Now," a male voice boomed from the doorway, "that is a sight worth coming home for!"

Mal turned without looking and flung himself into the arms of the man, causing him to rock back. Hannah and Abby followed suit and threw themselves at their father. So glad. So glad *Abba* was home. *Ima* stood back for a moment and watched with a smile. Then she went over to her husband and greeted him with a soft kiss on the lips.

****

Martha

… tried to enter her home with as little fanfare as possible; however, she could not manage to do so without garnering attention. Family life was in full swing. She had missed the rising of her older sisters (who swept by her with questioning looks), and all were now gone about their chores, tending their small flock and field with Father. This meant her absence wouldn't have gone unnoticed. What to do or how to explain? Mama stood looking at Martha's entrance with pursed lips and hands on her hips. Then she walked over to Martha and touched her face.

"Are you still feeling unwell?" Her voice was tinged with concern as she looked anxiously into the face of her daughter. Martha realized that Mama wasn't angry then. She'd astutely picked up that something had changed about her daughter, just not what.

"There is something I've been wanting to speak to you about," she continued before Martha could answer. She took Martha's hand in her own and drew her to the side. With a gesture of her other hand, she indicated that Martha should sit and drew her daughter down onto the woven mat. Martha was at a loss as to what was about to occur. Her mother seemed to be gathering herself, steeling herself for some event. Martha sat on the mat, rearranging her legs underneath. Mother placed a cup of *laban* in front of Martha as she took her seat and also handed her a bowl that had been set aside for Martha's meal.

Martha tore the *le-hhem* and stuffed it into her mouth, chewing voraciously. She was starved and only realized just how much when the food was placed in front of her. She pinched off the cheese and added figs to the mix, pocketing the food in her cheeks. Her mother should have wondered why, but as Martha took a gulp of the sour milk, she saw her mother, seemingly, compose herself in preparation. Then Martha, herself, began to wonder. What was all this about?

Puzzlement from Martha turned into concern and then absolute horror as she realized just what was happening. But she was powerless to stop it. Mother's face was set in determined lines. She had been strictly charged by her husband when he'd risen and noted Martha's absence. She took a deep breath to calm herself and began.

"There comes a time in every young girl's life ..."

Martha tried not to cringe.

****

Ari

... heard Shuey's voice singing over and over in his head until he couldn't get the silly song out of his head. Childish laughter punctuated each round.

Mal go bye, Ari go bye, Martha go bye. Giggle.

And then they were back home. Sent back home, rather, by Shuey himself. In reality, he was the Young Master as a child. Born into this world with that kind of power, not bequeathed as a gift, like Ari and the others. What troubles had he gotten into, at such a tender age while exercising his power? Ari smiled at that. And, he thought more soberly, had Shuey learned, like Mal, his responsibility to rein them in too late? Ari's mind was abuzz with activity, flying about, considering possible scenarios until a single thought brought his mind to a standstill.

He, Mal, and Martha had all assumed they were brought there, to young Shuey's time, to help, to aid in his escape. But the simple truth was he did not need their help. He was fully capable of wielding all the powers they displayed because they had been given by him. This meant he did not need them at all. Ari halted at the doorway to his home. So why? Why, then, were they taken there?

But before Ari could form the question, the answers came to him. Images of his father as a young man, getting to know his father in a way he never would, wonderful memories that were now

303

forever etched into his consciousness. *I shall go to him, but he shall not return to me,* said King David, upon hearing of the death of his son. Very true in Ari's case, too.

Ari also recalled the conversation had with the Young Master after they'd returned from their first adventure.

Can I see my father, he'd asked.

His time here is over, came the answer. The Young Master had not brought Ari's father back, but he'd allowed Ari to see his father again. Unbelievable love swelled in Ari as he realized the heart the Young Master must have for him and his pain. And he knew true gratitude as he felt the measure of what had been done for him. Surely not, just for him? But it felt like it.

His mother wordlessly handed him the clay water pitcher as he opened the door, extended from her folded arm. She met his eyes with an arched brow. Ari returned hers with a side smirk as he took the tendered vessel. He felt her eyes rake over him and held his breath, waiting for her judgment, to see if he passed inspection.

How was it that he suddenly looked so grown? Her son had matured before her eyes, and she had been blind to it. He was no longer a little boy. Pushing the pitcher aside, she gathered him into her arms.

"You are the son your father always wanted," she said to Ari. She touched her hand to his cheek fondly and looked into to gray eyes, so much like her Jules. His straight brows were like his father, in contrast to her softly curved brows, but one was raised in inquiry like she was so often wont to do. "He'd once met a boy, and was so taken with him. It was all he could talk about for years." She touched Ari's hair, similar to his father's in coloring, but coarse like her own in texture, as she remembered. Her eyes took on a dreamy quality.

"He always said he should like to have a son like him one day – the things he would teach him!"

Ari's arm went slack, holding the nearly forgotten water pitcher as he became caught up in her reverie. Visions of his father's many lessons, newly imported, assailed him again, and he heard Jules say, repeatedly: *One day, you may need to know this ...*

"Julius was so enamored of the young man," Mom continued, "he even named you after him." She finished with a small smile and patted his cheek, the moment over. She turned Ari in the direction he had come and gave him a little push. She needed water.

Ari walked out to the family cistern to complete his errand on wooden legs. His father, thanks to his blurting it out at the end, knew Ari was his child. He'd put the puzzle together and somehow figured out that he was raising that same

Ari. And maybe, even realized that he wouldn't be around to see Ari become a man.

Ari knew a few things, too. Like how his presence in the past, altered the future. His father, in this alternate life, still died but of different causes. Instead of falling victim to an accident, he perished early due to his heart giving out. And his father was destined to become centurion but again, for different reasons. Ari's expedition into the past changed everything, creating a ripple that affected him today. But Ari was comforted in knowing that Julius, too, had gotten the opportunity to meet the Young Master, albeit in child form. Ari didn't know why, but that thought made him glad.

"*Valē*, Father," Ari spoke into the sky, unsure of who he was talking to, or who was even listening. He just needed to say it. More than a mere hope or desire, it was a pledge that he would see his father again. Wishing he had thought of it at their parting,

Ari added a simple prayer that he recalled hearing his teachers read aloud from the holy scriptures:

The Lord watch between me and thee . . .

Epilogue

"Where will we go, Yosef?" Miriam inquired of her husband. Little Yeshua sat in her lap as she rode, clapping his hands and still singing his little made up song. She ruffled his hair affectionately. Yosef held the reins of the mule, leading them as they went. He looked in the direction of the sun, now setting. Their pace was unhurried because of the sure knowledge of who rode with them. It was he, of whom the prophecies foretold. God had shown them, once again, that all would be well concerning this child. Surely no harm could come to any of them, in light of what they'd just witnessed.

Still Yosef paid heed to the dream, not able to overlook it any longer. There were those still, who sought the life of their young son. And Yosef had seen with his own eyes the lengths they would go to in destroying his family. He held his hand up to shield his eyes from the dying light, squinting as he did.

309

"I suppose we could always go down to Egypt," he said to his wife as if the thought had just occurred to him. But in reality, Yosef recalled the admonition of his dream now, to go west, to the land of the Pharaohs. He was to stay there until the death of the current king of Judea. Only then would Yeshua be safe. He gave Miriam a small smile. "After all, our kind did well there, once before …"

"And was there until the death of Herod: that it might be fulfilled which was spoken of the Lord by the prophet, saying, Out of Egypt have I called my son." Matthew 2:15

Glossary

Abba – Father

gadol - big

Ima – Mother

klafta – Egyptian headdress

laban – a sour milk drink

le-hhem – bread

mētēr – Greek, mother

munifex – Latin, low ranking Roman soldier

neteru – Egyptian, angel

patér – Greek, father

Savta – grandmother

seh – lamb

ti anzeeb – Coptic (Egyptian), the school

toga – Roman style of dress

valē – Latin, goodbye or see you again

Italicized words are Hebrew unless otherwise noted
**All scripture references are KJV*

About L.G. Boyle

Her background includes Sunday school teacher, women's bible study leader, public speaker, choir director, and soloist. She is the mother of two children, both now adults. Raised the daughter of a Baptist minister, she has followed his legacy and created several ministries that flourished – bible study, praise team and singles ministries. She is a great fan of the Bible and loves to tell her own versions of the stories found therein. At the urging of friends, she began to write a blog, *The Word in My Life*, to encourage others by applying the scriptures to life events. This is the second book in the *Touched* series, and she anticipates sharing even more adventures with Ari, Mal, and Martha! Find out more about L.G. Boyle, her blog, and books at www.thewordinmylife.com

Made in the USA
Charleston, SC
24 July 2016